Second Summer
MacLarens of Fire Mountain Contemporary

SHIRLEEN DAVIES

Book One in the MacLarens of Fire Mountain

Contemporary Series

Books by Shirleen Davies

Historical Western Romance Series

MacLarens of Fire Mountain

Tougher than the Rest, Book One
Faster than the Rest, Book Two
Harder than the Rest, Book Three
Stronger than the Rest, Book Four
Deadlier than the Rest, Book Five
Wilder than the Rest, Book Six

Redemption Mountain

Redemption's Edge, Book One
Wildfire Creek, Book Two
Sunrise Ridge, Book Three
Dixie Moon, Book Four
Survivor Pass, Book Five

MacLarens of Boundary Mountain

Colin's Quest, Book One,
Brodie's Gamble, Book Two, Releasing 2016

Contemporary Romance Series

MacLarens of Fire Mountain

Second Summer, Book One
Hard Landing, Book Two
One More Day, Book Three
All Your Nights, Book Four
Always Love You, Book Five
Hearts Don't Lie, Book Six
No Getting Over You, Book Seven
'Til the Sun Comes Up, Book Eight, Releasing 2016

Peregrine Bay

Reclaiming Love, Book One, A Novella
Our Kind of Love, Book Two

The best way to stay in touch is to subscribe to my newsletter. Go to _www.shirleendavies.com_ and subscribe in the box at the top of the right column that asks for your email. You'll be notified of new books before they are released, have chances to win great prizes, and receive other subscriber-only specials.

For permission requests, contact the publisher.

Avalanche Ranch Press, LLC
PO Box 12618
Prescott, AZ 86304

Second Summer is a work of fiction. Names, characters, places, and incidents are either products of the author's imagination or used facetiously. Any resemblance to actual events, locales, or persons, living or dead, is wholly coincidental.

Cover artwork by The Killion Group

Book design and conversions by Joseph Murray at 3rdplanetpublishing.com

ISBN-10: 0989677346
ISBN-13: 978-0-9896773-4-9

Description

Second Summer – Book One in the MacLarens of Fire Mountain Contemporary Romance Series

In this passionate Contemporary Romance, author Shirleen Davies introduces her readers to the modern day MacLarens starting with Heath MacLaren, the head of the family. The Chairman of both the MacLaren Cattle Co. and MacLaren Land Development, he is a success professionally—his personal life is another matter.

Following a divorce after a long, loveless marriage Heath spends his time with women who are beautiful and passionate, yet unable to provide what he longs for . . .

Heath has never experienced love even though he witnesses it every day between his younger brother, Jace, and wife, Caroline. He wants what they have yet spends his time with women too young to understand what drives him and too focused on themselves to be true companions.

It's been two years since Annie's husband died, leaving her to build a new life. He was her soul-mate and confidante, she has no desire to find a replacement, yet longs for male friendship . . .

Annie's closest friend in Fire Mountain, Caroline MacLaren, is determined to see Annie come out of her shell after almost two years of mourning. A chance meeting with Heath turns into an offer to be a part of the MacLaren Foundation Board and an opportunity for a life outside her home sanctuary which has also become her prison. The platonic friendship that builds between Annie and Heath points to a future where each may rely on the other without the bonds a romance would entail.

However, without consciously seeking it, each yearns for more . . .

The MacLaren Development Company is booming with Heath at the helm. His meetings at a partner company with the young, beautiful marketing director, who makes no secret of her desire for him, are a temptation. But is she the type of woman he truly wants?

Annie's acceptance of the deep, yet passionless, friendship with Heath sustains her, lulling her to believe it is all she needs. At least until Heath drops a bombshell, forcing Annie to realize that what she took for friendship is actually a deep, lasting love. One she doesn't want to lose.

Each must decide to settle—or fight for it all.

Second Summer is the first book in the MacLarens of Fire Mountain Contemporary series—heartwarming stories of difficult choices, loyalty, and lasting romance. Watch for Hard Landing in the Spring of 2014.

Dedication

This book is dedicated to Richard, the love of my life.

Acknowledgements

Thanks also to my editor and proofreader, Deborah Gunn, and all of my beta readers. Their insights and suggestions are greatly appreciated.

Finally, many thanks to my wonderful resources, including Diane Lebow, who has been a whiz at guiding my social media endeavors, my cover designer, idrewdesign, and Joseph Murray who is a whiz at formatting my books for both print and electronic versions.

Second Summer

Second Summer

Chapter One

Late January

Annie walked into the crowded room, making her way between men in jeans and cowboy boots, and those dressed in suits—and cowboy boots. She passed waiters with trays balanced precariously on one hand while using the other to distribute champagne, wine, and non-alcoholic punch to people who barely acknowledged their presence while accepting the free libations.

She'd been there thirty minutes and had yet to see the friend who'd invited her. It was Annie's first venture into adult society since her husband had died almost two years ago after a gallant battle against cancer. Annie and Kit had been a very social couple. He'd laugh if he knew she hadn't been to an event of any kind since he'd died. Kit wouldn't know that her heart had been buried with him.

Her path had taken her in a jagged route from one side of the room to the other, but still, no sign of her friend. Annie was just about to give up when she heard a familiar voice.

"Annie! Over here!"

She turned to see her closest friend in Fire Mountain, Caroline MacLaren, wave her over. Caroline had badgered her for weeks to come to the charity event that she chaired. It was for foster children and she knew it was one of Annie's heart-points. Kit and Annie had been active in a couple of organizations dedicated to improving the foster care program and establishing funding programs for teens who'd turned eighteen and were about to be cut-loose from government support even if they were only weeks or months from obtaining their high school diploma. Sometimes their foster parents allowed them to stay, but sometimes not. It was a broken system that broke Annie's heart— at least what was now left of it. Without Kit, the fire had slowed even if she still continued to write checks to the programs they'd supported.

"I've looked all over for you," Caroline said as she hooked her arm through Annie's and kissed her cheek. "Where were you hiding?"

"I was on the other side of the room. It's a much larger crowd than I remembered." Annie looked at the four other people in the circle. She'd met Annie's husband, Jace, but the other two were unfamiliar.

"Annie, this is my brother-in-law, Heath MacLaren, and his date, Jennifer. Of course, you already know Jace."

"Annie, it's good to see you again," Jace bent down and placed a quick kiss on her cheek.

"It's nice to be out again, Jace." Annie's gaze shifted to the other couple.

"Annie, it's a pleasure. I've heard a lot of good things about you." Heath MacLaren held out a hand. Annie grasped it for a brief moment. His hand was large, warm, and welcoming, the way Kit's had been the first time she'd met him. She shook the thought from her mind.

"Nice to meet you also, Heath."

"Hello, Annie. Glad you could join us. Caroline mentioned you used to be very involved in this group." Jennifer was tall, slender, with stunning golden red hair that fell in waves below her shoulders. To say she was stunning was a gross understatement. She looked like a runway model in her sequined, emerald green evening gown.

"Yes, I used to be quite involved. Perhaps I will again at some point." Annie had thought tonight would be the catalyst she needed to get her life going again. Now she wasn't so sure. Had it always seemed so hard to move through these circles or had she become jaded?

They all turned at the sound of the maître d' announcing that dinner was served. The lights flickered twice before the guests started towards the dining room door. Her group was directed to a table for eight. The other couple and single guest were already seated when the five of them arrived. They were in the front at a center table. Annie was shown a seat next to an older gentleman who appeared to be soloing it just like her. He stood to pull out her chair.

"Seth Garner," he said and held out a hand which Annie accepted.

"Hello Seth. I'm Annie Sinclair."

"Ah, another Scot, Heath. Did you know that?" Seth harassed.

"Yes, as a matter of fact I did." Heath settled in his chair on the other side of Annie. "Are you of Scottish descent or is that your married name?"

A pain so quick, yet so deep cut through Annie before she had time to think. She drew in a short breath. After almost two years the mention of her loss still hurt. "Both, actually. My husband was half Scottish. I'm perhaps a fourth. No one will admit to more," she smiled, hoping it would disguise her unease.

"Hah, she's got you there," Seth joked.

"And you, Heath, are you a full Scot or another mixed breed?"

"Oh, at this point in our lives I believe most of us are a jigsaw of backgrounds. However, I will admit to the majority of my genes being Scot." He smiled, and for the first time in two years Annie felt a jolt to her heart that had nothing to do with pain.

The dinner passed as most of these events did with more wine, introductions, announcements, rich desserts, too strong coffee, and a live auction. The largest donation was an all-inclusive two-week trip for two to Paris. The accommodations could be used for up to two years in the future, which gave the recipient plenty of time to plan. It was purchased by Heath MacLaren.

With the announcements over, the band was free to begin. Annie and Kit had liked to dance. Nothing fancy like some of their friends but they'd had fun. The band tonight played a mix of pop,

4

country, some hip-hop, and a few big band numbers. They had been brought in from Phoenix just for this event and the crowd loved them.

Seth had danced with Annie. He was a good dancer, kept the conversation going, and was a gentleman—three qualities Annie admired. He'd excused himself to join a group of men on the other side of the room, while the other couples visited with friends.

Now she sat alone at the table, sipping her wine, waiting for an appropriate time to say her goodbyes. It was almost eleven, way past time for her to be home in bed with a book.

Annie turned to place her empty glass on the table and push herself up when she felt a hand on her shoulder.

"May I have this dance, Annie?"

She looked up to see Heath's intense green eyes fix on her.

"I was just getting ready to leave."

"Just one dance."

She listened to what the band was playing. It was a fast number. Yes, she could do this.

"All right." She stood to take his hand just as the song ended. They both looked toward the stage when a beautiful, slow song started. Annie turned to Heath. He must have seen the hesitancy in her gaze because he grasped her hand tighter and led her toward the dance floor.

Turning her toward him, Heath took Annie in a gentle embrace, and began to move to the music. After a while he felt her relax. He was glad he'd asked her. Caroline had shared some of what had happened, but he was certain there was more to the story. His sister-in-law was discreet and exceedingly loyal to her family and friends. He knew she thought of Annie as a close friend. Funny that she'd never introduced her to him before.

It was a soft, romantic song, and Heath was a good lead. He was taller than she'd first thought, at over six feet. Her five-foot-five height was a stretch even with her three-inch heels. She hated wearing heels, but tonight she was glad to have them on.

So this was Heath, Annie thought. Caroline hadn't told her too much about him, but had always warned her away. His situation was *complicated* Caroline had said. She had told Annie he'd been married for a long time to a woman he'd met in high school. Annie assumed it was the standard marriage of high-school sweethearts gone wrong as the two matured, but Caroline had almost snorted when Annie had used that phrase. She knew he had a reputation for being seen with a different woman at each event he attended, even if all were stunning, tall, and, according to Caroline, ten to fifteen years his junior. At least now she had a face to put with a name.

The song ended but Heath didn't let loose his hold, at least not right away. She pulled back and looked up. Those green eyes focused on her again, and a slight smile curved his lips. "Thank you, Annie Sinclair. That was very nice."

She smiled in return. "Yes, Heath, it was. Thanks so much for asking me."

He led her back to the table, picked up her small clutch, and handed it to Annie.

"I'll help you get your coat."

"But I should say goodbye to Caroline."

"I'll tell her for you. Come on." Heath took her elbow and led her to the coat room then walked her outside to her car.

"Thank you, but I could've walked out by myself. You still have Jennifer inside, waiting."

"It was my pleasure. Besides, Jennifer can entertain herself quite well without me." Heath took her keys and unlocked the door. "Well, goodnight, Annie. Have a safe drive home."

"Goodnight, Heath." Annie slid into the seat and started the engine.

Heath made a brief wave and was off, back to his date, and, well, whatever gorgeous, single men did on a night like this.

Annie drove home. The car radio would normally be playing in the background while she wrestled with one thought or another, but not tonight. Tonight her mind wandered to the last dance and how glad she was that Caroline had encouraged her to attend.

She felt as if she'd crossed a giant hurdle. Annie felt a little lighter as she pulled into her drive and punched the garage door button. It was as if a small piece of a large burden had been lifted, simply pulled away.

She changed into her favorite sweats and sat on the floor to stretch. It was a routine she'd had for years along with using her home gym three times a week. After a while she felt tired enough to slide under the covers. Her thoughts went again to the dinner and table guests. Seth had been very attentive. She'd danced with Jace and the other gentleman at the table, and finally with Heath.

Annie drifted off, hearing the last song in her head, and feeling better than she had in a long time.

Chapter Two

March, two months later...

Annie woke to a glaring sun shining in from her large bedroom window. She'd gotten home so late she hadn't even remembered to close the curtains. Her bedroom looked out over a large deck and an acre of tall pines. She loved this place—had from the first moment she'd seen it.

It hadn't been Kit's first choice, but they'd looked at so many houses by the time they'd seen this one he would have taken anything she wanted. His first choice was five acres ten miles outside of town, and miles from the private airport where he kept the plane. After a few days of soul-searching, he'd come to the decision that the one-story ranch two miles from town and five from the airport was perfect.

Annie started for the kitchen, and coffee, when she heard her cell phone. She checked the caller I.D.

"Hello, Caroline." She balanced the phone between her shoulder and ear while putting the coffee in the little container, shutting the lid, and pushing the start button.

"Hi. I heard it was a real late night getting everything set."

"Yes it was and I need to be at the church by eight o'clock. The bus arrives at eight thirty.

Anyway, I'll sleep when this is all over." Annie watched the water drip from the machine into her cup. She really needed coffee this morning.

"You're right about that. Jace and I'll be there about eight-fifteen. Anything you need us to pick up on the way?"

"Nope, I think it's all covered at this point. See you in a bit." Annie hung up, walked toward the bedroom, sipped the hot coffee, and grimaced—she'd forgotten the sweetener. She back-tracked and grabbed one packet. *Slow down*, she told herself, there was plenty of time.

Annie pulled her small SUV into the church lot right at eight, turned off the engine, and sat. She mentally checked off everything one more time to be sure nothing had been missed, then climbed out and strolled to the office.

"Hi, Claire. Everything ready?" she asked and set down her notepad.

"Hi, Annie. As far as I know it's all good." She looked out the window. "Looks like your bus is here early. Good thing because some of the kids have been here for an hour."

Annie walked to the community room and peered inside. About twelve kids were sitting around, listening to music, watching television, or texting. About twenty-eight more from various foster families had signed up for the field trip to Flagstaff. Many hadn't been out of Fire Mountain in years. For some it was their first trip beyond the community of a hundred thousand.

"Annie," Claire called, "I'll go speak to the driver if you want to check off the rest of the kids as they arrive."

Annie grabbed the clipboard, made sure all the current kids were checked off, and walked outside. She peered at her watch, eight-fifteen. She looked up to see Caroline's large, silver SUV pull into the lot. Caroline jumped down, followed by Jace on the other side. As Annie started to focus on some newcomers in another car she spotted one more occupant step out of the SUV—Heath.

Annie hadn't seen him since the charity event, and certainly hadn't expected him to show up as one of the chaperones for the field trip. Caroline had always told her how busy he was between the various businesses and his social life.

"Hey, Annie!" Caroline waved and started towards her. "Brought an extra chaperone. Hope it's okay."

"Of course it is. We can always use the extra help. Hello, Heath. Haven't seen you in a while." She shielded her eyes from the early morning sun and looked up. Yep. He was just as handsome as she remembered.

"Hello, Annie. I think the last time was the charity dinner," Heath lied. He knew exactly the last time he'd seen her, had wanted to call her numerous times, but always stopped himself. Besides, as Caroline's friend, she was off-limits.

"Yes, well, it's good to have you here. Would you and Jace mind rounding up the kids as they arrive and show them into the community room?

Caroline and I need to speak with the parents and sponsors." She handed him the clipboard.

"I'm here for whatever you need," Heath replied and followed Jace toward the parking lot.

Annie stepped back to allow them to walk past her towards a group of kids about fifty feet away. Heath's chambray shirt was tucked into tight fitting jeans, which covered work-worn brown cowboy boots. She'd only seen him twice—once at the charity dinner and then today. He'd worn the traditional cowboy hat each time. He looked good.

"Won't be long, maybe twenty minutes and everyone will be loaded and ready to go. You sure it was all right to bring Heath?" Caroline had walked up to stand beside her.

"Of course, why wouldn't it be?" She'd never said a word to her friend about the attraction she felt toward Heath. Annie knew all single women were attracted to him, and many married women as well. It would have been a ridiculous conversation to have with her closest friend in Fire Mountain. After all, the MacLarens had helped settle this area. Their ancestors had been mayors, councilmen, state representatives, and held numerous other local offices over the years. They were a public icon and Caroline was a part of it. Anyway, it was just a passing feeling after being alone for almost two years. She would've felt the same if any attractive man had paid attention to her.

"Well, I know he kept an eye on you at the dinner." Caroline held up a hand when Annie started to protest. "I know you never said anything, but I got the impression you liked the attention he gave you."

"Of course I enjoyed it. Any woman would be flattered to have Heath pay her any attention at all. He's good-looking, smart, funny, and a great dancer, by the way. But it was one dance and he walked me to my car. Nothing more. Besides, I've had the love of my life, and believe me, I don't expect it to happen twice."

"Just making sure. You know he's asked about you a few times."

"What?"

"Heath never pays any attention to my friends. You're the first."

Annie mulled this over a moment before shaking her head. "Caroline, believe me, that doesn't mean a thing. The man's got women hanging off him like tinsel. Besides, you warned me off of him, remember?" She was saved from Caroline's reply when the driver stood on the bus steps and waved to them. "Looks like it's time to go."

The group arrived in Flagstaff almost two hours later, parking in the large university lot. Caroline and Annie had taken seats in the front while other chaperones had sat in the middle. Jace and Heath had taken seats in the far back, which allowed them time to talk as well as keep watch on the kids. All were teens in their sophomore, junior, or senior year in high school. They'd all expressed an interest in seeing the large campus in northern Arizona.

Planning for the field trip had taken a great deal of time, and somewhere along the way Annie had forgotten that the MacLarens funded a foundation to help pay tuition and housing expenses for foster children who went to two or four-year colleges. Caroline, Jace, and Heath were all on the board, as well as a couple of local businessmen. They wanted to be involved, get to know the kids who'd be moving out, going on their own. It suddenly made sense why Heath had come on the trip.

"What's first?" Jace asked. Heath stood beside him, looking over the vast campus while the other chaperones crowded around.

"A couple of administrators will give us a tour and explain admittance procedures. Two of the oldest foster kids have already applied, so they'll have individual attention from counselors. The rest will tour some of the outlying buildings then we'll meet back at the cafeteria for lunch." Annie had been reading from her itinerary, not noticing that Heath followed her every word. "We need to split into two groups, one with each administrator."

A couple of the adults took on the task of dividing the kids and adults. They'd finished just as the two school officials arrived.

"We're all set," Annie informed the new arrivals.

The first group took off in one direction while Annie's group went another. She'd expected to see Caroline in her group, but when she looked behind her it was Heath her eyes locked on.

"I thought you'd want to stay with Jace." Annie had dropped back a couple of steps to come even with Heath.

"You did, huh?" he grinned.

She studied him. Was he teasing or just making conversation? "Doesn't matter, we'll all see the same things." Annie tore her gaze from Heath to concentrate on their guides.

The group walked through a dorm, then the student activity center, and the library. Heath kept pace with Annie the entire time, making small talk, not crowding her, just staying close enough to make her aware of his presence. She didn't know what it was about the man that had her on edge. She had no interest in a relationship, wasn't looking for anyone to help her fill her time. Her life was good as it was.

"How have you been? Caroline mentioned it's been almost two years since your husband's death." Heath regretted the comment immediately. He looked down at her but Annie's face was impassive.

"I'm doing good. Everything seems to be falling back into place." She glanced toward a student who'd asked a question, then back at Heath. "It will be two years next month. April eighth. At one in the afternoon." She swallowed, trying to get past the lump in her throat.

"He was a good man, a loss for everyone who knew him."

"You knew my husband?" Annie hadn't known that Kit and Heath were acquaintances.

"We were members of the same men's group that met downtown for lunch a couple of times a month. Looking back, I wish I'd spent more time around Kit. He was an interesting man."

"That he was. There'll never be another like him."

The sadness in Annie's voice wasn't lost on Heath. He realized how much she still loved her deceased husband and wondered if that kind of pain ever healed.

The rest of the day passed according to the schedule allowing them time to walk the old downtown area, the original train station, and stop in a few shops. Most of the kids had some spending money, but it was obvious that others had been given nothing. Jace and Heath passed out a twenty-dollar bill to each one, not differentiating between who had money and who didn't. Now they all had something.

She'd been told that the MacLarens were generous, and today was just another example of their kindness.

The ride home was uneventful. Caroline sat with Jace while Heath took a seat across the aisle from Annie. He'd been quiet since their exchange about her husband.

Heath stared out the bus window, thinking over the conversation they'd had about Kit. He'd been honest when he'd said Kit was a good man.

What Heath hadn't mentioned to Annie was her husband's clear devotion to her. From the few conversations they'd shared, it was obvious that Kit adored his wife. Heath had found himself wondering what his life would've been like if he'd loved a woman the way Kit had.

He glanced across the aisle at Annie's profile. She was attractive—not what he'd consider stunning. He'd spent the last few years dating women who were beautiful and younger. Caroline had said her friend was a few years older than her, about Heath's age, which was forty-five. The women he dated were closer to thirty, maybe thirty-five, but rarely older than that. They understood he had no interest in love or a relationship. After years in a loveless marriage he had no desire to be entangled in anything permanent.

Annie was what his friend Dale would call a keeper. Someone you'd fall in love with, marry, and come home to every night. That wasn't something Heath wanted. But he did find himself wondering if he could be friends with someone like her. *Could a man enjoy a woman's company, become good friends, without it becoming physical?*

Could he?

Chapter Three

"What do you think?" Caroline asked after she'd enumerated the reasons she wanted to bring Annie on as a board member of their foundation. They needed another outside member, one that had a passion for foster children, and could provide additional input. The current board consisted of Heath, Jace, Caroline, their attorney, and their accountant. Annie would be a good fit.

"Have you spoken with her about this?" Jace asked.

"No, not yet. I wanted to pass it by all of you first."

"She does have a good background, firsthand knowledge of the foster care system, and an obvious desire to help the kids. Do you think she'd be interested?" Colt Minton had been the MacLaren attorney for years, as had his father, grandfather, and great-grandfather. He'd grown up with Health and Jace, knew their interest in the community and desire to give back.

"I believe so but I don't want to speak with her until we've reached a decision."

"Does she work, Caroline?" Colt asked.

"She's a writer. Quite good, in fact. That keeps her busy but her time is flexible—perfect for a position on our board."

Heath had busied himself reviewing another item on their agenda, concealing his thoughts on Annie joining the board, but lifted his gaze at Caroline's mention of Annie's work. He'd never thought of her working.

"I think it's a good idea. What about you, Heath?" Jace looked at his brother, wondering why he hadn't participated in the conversation. As the foundation chairman, he was normally quite candid in his thoughts and questions.

"I've met her just the two times, so I'll defer to you and Caroline on this one. However, we've discussed adding one more person who can add diverse opinions and ideas. Someone with connections to possible donors and funding sources. As a writer, perhaps she could help guide our grant proposals."

"She knows a lot of people but I don't believe she'd be the ultimate lead for funding. I do think she'd be great for guiding our grant efforts." Caroline knew Annie had performed a similar role in past organizations and would be a huge benefit to them in that area.

"Well, if we're done with talking, let's move this forward," Jace recommended.

A minute later they had unanimously approved their new board member and instructed Caroline to discuss with Annie their desire to have her join them.

After the meeting everyone stood and left— except Heath. He had mixed emotions about Annie. It had been a week since the field trip and each day he'd thought of her. He knew for a fact he'd never date her, but couldn't shake the desire he felt to pull her into his life in some way. Perhaps this was the opportunity he needed to get to know her better. Even though he was busy with work, family, and an active social life, there was still a void he'd never been able to fill. Not after marrying, not after the birth of his children, and definitely not with the women he dated.

He tapped the pencil on the pad a couple of times, laid it down on the paper, and sat back. There was so much more he had to accomplish today. Instead, he found himself wondering if Annie would accept their offer to join the board. He was surprised to realize how much he hoped she would.

******

"Oh, Caroline, I just don't know," Annie sat on a kitchen stool, drinking hot tea with Caroline sitting next to her, staring. Annie couldn't miss the excitement in her friend's eyes.

"What's not to know? This is perfect for you and for the board. You'd be great at it and you have the time. If it's the expense..."

"No, it's not the expense. I understand the board reimburses foundation expenses. That's not the issue."

"Then what?"

"I'm not sure." Annie thought a minute trying to pinpoint the exact reason she was pushing back. "You're all so accomplished and understand what's needed in a program of this size. What could I possibly add?"

"Are you kidding? You're the only one who's experienced the foster system first hand."

"That was years ago."

"Granted, but that's still more knowledge than the rest of us. Plus, you've written grants before and succeeded in obtaining additional funding. You know the players and who to call."

"Caroline that was in California, not Arizona. Most of the funding organization decision makers have changed since I wrote grants. It takes time to reestablish contacts. It's a long process."

Caroline sat, watching Annie, knowing she was considering the offer. She slid off her stool and walked around the worktable where they sat. She grabbed the kettle and poured more hot water for herself and Annie, understanding her friend needed time.

"How much time would it require?"

"We meet once a month for about two hours. Then whatever time you need to start reconnecting with the grant organizations. There is administrative help for you. MacLaren Cattle Co. will make available whatever resources you need."

Annie thought over the offer. It was something she would normally jump at. Programs to help foster children were her passion, this was perfect for her. Why was she stalling?

"All right. If you think I'd benefit the board, then yes, I'd be honored to accept."

Caroline grabbed Annie into a warm hug then stepped back.

"I'm so glad! You'll love it." Caroline glanced at her watch. "I'd better get going. Still need to make a couple of stops before heading home. I'll get you the past board minutes and anything else you need sometime this week. Oh, and don't forget you're meeting us at the shooting range tomorrow. Three o'clock."

"I remember. See you tomorrow."

Annie sat at the kitchen counter after Caroline left, holding her cup between her hands, and wondering what she'd gotten herself into. She knew it was just what was needed to get her life back on track. Handling the field trips helped, but this was the opportunity she'd wanted since she'd learned of the foundation. The issue wasn't the additional time or work needed to fulfill her role. The issue was the chairman.

She'd thought of him numerous times since the field trip. He was a compelling figure, one of those men who commanded attention and respect, but also something more.

Her life had settled into a routine she enjoyed, one she understood—writing, friends, and family. They'd had three children—two boys and a girl. One boy and girl was from Kit's previous marriage and a boy from theirs. The oldest boy was now out of college and working in northern California, the daughter was in grad school in San Diego, and the youngest boy was finishing up his degree in Los Angeles. Each called at least once a week and texted every couple of days. They were doing well, adjusting to the loss of their father, and understanding of her desire to stay in Fire

Mountain and not return to California—except for occasional family gatherings at her second home in San Juan Capistrano. They were a close family. Her life was full. Now that she had this new position on the board, there was nothing else she needed.

Her cell phone buzzed on the counter. She glanced at a local number she didn't recognize and picked it up.

"Hello."

"Annie?"

"Yes."

"It's Heath MacLaren. I just heard from Caroline and wanted to let you know how pleased we are that you accepted. I hope you feel the same."

"Yes, I'm very excited, and honored, Heath. Thanks so much."

"It's our pleasure. Tell you what, I'm heading into town in about two hours. Meet me for a drink to celebrate your acceptance at Stanton's. Say five o'clock?"

Annie didn't want to say yes, yet she didn't want to say no, either. It would be a good idea to get to know Heath better. After all, he was the chairman of the foundation and Caroline's brother-in-law. "That would be fine. I'll meet you there."

"I'll look forward to it." The line went dead.

She stared at the phone, then closed it, walking down the hall to her small gym. A good workout was just what she needed before the meeting at Stanton's.

******

"Annie, over here." Heath sat at a corner table, lifting his hand so she could see him. Next to him sat a very pretty woman with short dark hair.

"Glad you could make it. This is Laurel, a friend of mine."

Annie extended a hand. "It's a pleasure, Laurel."

"Same here, Annie. Heath just told me you'd been elected to their board. Congratulations." She turned to Heath. "It was good to see you. Call me when you have some time." Laurel placed a quick kiss on Heath's cheek and stood.

"See you, Annie."

"Laurel." Annie watched the young woman walk away. Even though it was in the fifties outside, she wore a thin sheath about eight inches above her knees, and heels that had to be at least three inches high. Annie turned her gaze back to Heath and noticed his eyes were still following Laurel out the door.

"Nice girl," Annie said and sat down across from Heath.

"Uh, yes." Heath hadn't meant for Annie to walk into the restaurant to see him with one of the women he'd been seeing. He'd gone out with Laurel a few times. She was nice but as far from someone like Annie as you could get. "What would you like?"

"Scotch, neat, would be great." She enjoyed the look of surprise on Heath's face, but he recovered quickly and ordered the drink, which came within minutes.

He picked up his glass. "To your membership on our board." Heath tilted his glass toward Annie. She responded in kind and took a sip, letting the liquid ease down her throat, warming her as it went.

"So, tell me exactly why you think I'd be an asset to the board." Annie studied the remaining scotch in her glass then set it on the table. She sat back, relaxing for the first time since she'd walked into Stanton's.

Heath studied her. She certainly got to the point. He liked and admired that in a person. "Your background, actually. None of us have had the experience in the foster care system that you've had. We don't know first-hand how the kids feel—what they fear or expect. Plus, Caroline told us you've written grants before. That's a big issue for us as we want the foundation to stand on its own at some point."

Annie stared at her glass before taking another swallow. She hadn't had scotch since Kit died. Another step for her.

"Yes, I was in the system from the time I was ten until I was eighteen. That was years ago, and in California, so I don't know how comparable the experience is to what the kids go through now."

"Needs don't really change from one generation to another, do they?" Heath asked.

"No, I guess they don't." She thought back to her time as a foster child. "The biggest issues for me were security and getting an education. I wasn't looking to be loved as much as I wanted to be accepted. Moving through the system without falling behind was important to me."

"And did that happen?"

"I was one of the fortunate ones. My foster family was wonderful, they're still almost like parents. There was no way they could afford to adopt me, but they provided a good home and as much support as they could. They let me stay after I turned eighteen, which was four months before my high school graduation. The money stopped but I worked after school and weekends, and gave them almost everything I made. It was a good experience, much better than many in the system."

Heath had heard all types of stories from foster children since the MacLarens had started the foundation. Somehow hearing it from an adult made it all the more real. His home had been nothing like Annie's experience. He had so many questions. Didn't she have relatives willing to take her in? Were there siblings? Was she only with the one family? He'd heard some heart-breaking stories over the years and found himself hoping Annie hadn't had any of those experiences.

"Were there other children in the family?"

"Yes, but they were older, out of college. They treated me well. I don't keep in touch with them much, not like I do their parents."

Heath signaled the waiter for another drink, then sat back, absorbed in her story.

"How'd you meet Kit?"

"He went to the same church as my foster parents. Kit was older and already married when

we met. I just thought of him as a nice, older man."
Annie smiled at the recollection.

"Older man, huh? How much older?"

"Twelve years. It seemed like so much more when I was sixteen. We met each other again a few years later. His wife had suffered with cancer for a couple of years then passed away the year before I saw him again. For some reason I didn't see him as older by that time. We married several months later."

Twelve years seemed quite a distance between their ages. Heath sobered when it hit him that Laurel was fifteen years younger than him. Maybe that wasn't such a stretch if it was with the right person and both wanted something permanent.

"Do you have children?" Heath asked.

"Oh yes. Three. Kit had a boy and girl when we met. Then we had a son—he'll graduate from USC the end of next year. The truth is, they're all mine. Cameron and Brooke were young when Kit and I married. I've been with them most of their lives. Eric is twenty. I don't believe the oldest two ever think about having a different mother than Eric. It just doesn't come up." Annie rested her head back and followed the glowing stained glass chandelier that rotated slowly from the ceiling. Blue, green, burgundy, and gold that threw colored shadows across the table. "What about you, Heath? Caroline told me you were divorced but she never spoke of children."

Heath smiled at the thought of Trey and Cassie. "Yes. My daughter Cassandra, Cassie, is eighteen, and Trey is twenty-three. He graduated from the Naval Academy and is now in pilot training. Cassie graduates in a couple of months from high school and will probably head off to ASU in the fall."

"It must be hard having Trey so far away and Cassie with her mother much of the time."

"Oh, she lives with me, not her mother. Pamela lives in Scottsdale and Cassie has no desire to move to the valley. Not that her mother showed must interest in having Cassie with her."

"Sorry, I just assumed you must split custody. I didn't mean to pry." Caroline had never shared any details of Heath's life with Annie other than that he was divorced and dated quite a number of women.

"No problem. I have custody, which works well for everyone. My life is great and the kids are doing fine. The divorce had been coming for years. It's better this way." Heath threw back the last of his Jameson's and looked at his watch. "Well, I hate to leave but I have an appointment. Thanks for meeting me on the spur of the moment."

There was still one finger of scotch left in Annie's glass. She stood and extended her hand to Heath. "My pleasure and thanks for the drink."

Heath accepted her hand in a warm grip then bent forward to place a kiss on her cheek. He stepped back. "What are you doing the day after tomorrow?"

"Saturday?"

"Yes, we're going on a trail ride. Why don't you join us?"

"Well, I..."

"There are plenty of horses to choose from and any of the tack you need. We ride out at eight in the morning. Be there by seven-thirty." He glanced at his watch again. "Got to run. See you on Saturday."

Chapter Four

Annie sat on her bed staring at the clock, debating whether or not to set the alarm for five o'clock. He hadn't waited for her acceptance, just assumed she'd show up. It irritated her while at the same time amused her. Caroline had said he was a take-charge kind of guy.

She'd spoken with Caroline earlier that day at the gun range where Annie was taking lessons. Annie confirmed that Caroline and Jace would be on the ride along with Heath's daughter, Cassie. If Caroline and Jace's sons, Blake and Brett were interested, they would join them.

Annie loved to ride. She and Kit owned two horses which she boarded a couple of miles from her home. Her gelding, Rascal, was a chestnut quarter horse. He stood fifteen hands and Annie made every effort to ride him at least once a week. She still owned Kit's grey gelding, Picasso. Annie just hadn't had the heart to sell him. She'd made an arrangement a year ago with a young man just back from overseas who'd exited the Army. He loved to ride but didn't own a horse. He rode both a couple of times a week for a small monthly payment from Annie. It was a great deal for both of them.

She figured it would be fun to ride another horse, see different trails. Besides, she and

Caroline had only had about an hour yesterday and that was consumed with a discussion of the board appointment plus their time at the range today. Tomorrow they'd have time to talk.

Annie reached over and set the alarm.

******

"You sure she can ride, Caroline?" Heath asked for the second time.

"Yes. I've already told you about her horses. Don't worry. She'll let you know if Gremlin's too much for her."

Gremlin was a palomino gelding with real personality. At four he was still frisky but well trained.

"Tell me again who Annie is, Aunt Caroline?" Cassie walked up with her horse.

"She's a very good friend of mine and we just voted her onto the board of the foundation. You'll love her." Caroline finished saddling Gremlin then walked him over by her horse at the same time Annie's car pulled up by the house. "Hey, Annie! We're over here," Caroline called.

Heath stopped what he was doing to watch Annie get out of her car. She looked taller, sleeker, in her tight fitting jeans and blouse.

"She looks a little old for you, Dad," Cassie teased. She'd been in a restaurant downtown when her father had walked in with a woman who looked like she was twenty. Cassie hadn't been able to hide her surprise at her father's choice of dates.

Turned out the woman was twenty-nine, still way too young in Cassie's mind.

"I am not dating Annie if that's what you're thinking. She's a friend of your aunt's and now on our board. That's it. Now, behave," Heath threw out but in jest not anger.

Annie waved back, grabbed her hat, gloves, and jacket then starting walking toward the barn. She came up beside Caroline and gave her a brief hug.

"Annie, this is Heath's daughter, Cassie."

"Hello, Cassie. It's a pleasure to meet you." Annie extended her hand, which the young woman accepted.

"Hi, Annie. Dad says you're riding with us today. That's the horse he selected." She pointed to Gremlin.

Annie turned toward a beautiful palomino. "Oh, he's gorgeous." She walked over to the horse and ran her hand over his neck and back. "What's his name?"

"Gremlin." Heath stood a couple of feet away, watching her. Her boots were sturdy and well worn, and she'd brought gloves. Maybe she would be okay.

"Oh, hello, Heath."

"Annie. I wasn't sure you'd come."

"Well, I wasn't sure either to be truthful. I usually ride my horse, Rascal, on Saturday mornings, but I wanted to see more of the ranch, and catch up with Caroline. Thanks for the invitation."

"No problem." He saw Jace walk up with his horse. "Looks like we're ready." He turned back to Annie. "You need a boost?"

"Nope, I think I can make it." Annie did a quick check of the cinch, slipped into her gloves, and mounted in one slow, easy move. She'd brought a baseball cap with an Arizona Diamondbacks logo, instead of the more traditional cowboy hat. It held tighter when she rode at speed.

"Are you a baseball fan?" Cassie asked.

"Yes, I am. As well as football. I enjoy watching ice hockey also. You?"

"All three plus basketball. Dad has season tickets to everything. Maybe you can go with him sometime."

Heath had ridden up beside them, hearing the last comment. "You're welcome anytime, Annie. I have four to each game. Get ahold of Caroline and she'll set you up. Most games are pretty open." He nudged his horse, Blackjack, toward Jace. "You set?"

"Yep, let's go."

Annie, with Cassie and Caroline on either side, rode behind Jace and Heath. It gave all three a chance to talk while the men decided the destination. Two hours later they took a turn up one of the small hills, rode down the other side, then into a canyon before stopping.

Heath ground tied Blackjack and looked toward the women. He'd glanced behind him several times during the ride to be sure Annie kept up. Caroline was right—her friend was a solid rider.

"Who's got the trail mix?" Jace shouted toward the women. He pulled out water bottles from his saddlebag and distributed them to each person.

"As if the man didn't know who carried the food," Caroline said and pulled out two bags of her husband's favorite snack plus fruit. "Here you go." She tossed a bag to Jace and kept the other for the women who'd chosen a group of large boulders to lean against.

"It's so beautiful out here. How many acres do you have?" Annie asked no one in particular.

"Over five hundred thousand in three states for our cattle operations. Another several thousand reserved for horse breeding and training programs. We concentrate on quarter and cutting horses." Heath leaned a hip against a nearby rock and scanned the horizon. They'd all worn heavy jackets as the March temperatures were still in the forties much of the time. If they continued higher they might still find some snow. He doubted there'd be more this year, but you never knew.

The large amount of acreage surprised Annie. "I had no idea it was that large. It must take all of your time as well as Jace's to run it."

"Not so much anymore. It's set up like any large corporation with a management team who handle all the aspects of a large-scale cattle operation. Everything is more scientific nowadays than it was a hundred and fifty years ago when it was started."

"Has it always been in MacLaren hands?"

"It has. One generation after the next. I'm hopeful Trey, after his stint in the Navy, and Cassie will want to continue, along with Jace and Caroline's children. We've been fortunate. Most large ranches are owned by corporations that are far removed from the founding families."

They relaxed in silence a while longer before Annie's curiosity kicked in again.

"What parts of the business do you spend your time on?"

"I'm still the chairman of the cattle operations. We have a president that actually handles day-to-day decisions. Jace heads up the horse breeding division. My focus is now on our development company. High-end housing, some middle and lower end, plus hospitality and retail sites. I travel a lot as we own properties throughout Arizona, New Mexico, and Nevada, plus a few in Colorado. Keeps me busy."

"And out of trouble?" Annie joked.

"Well, not so much," Heath's grin lit his face.

"You just gonna gab all morning or are we going to ride on for lunch?" Jace walked up with Caroline and Cassie.

"We're ready when you are," Heath replied, walked to his horse, and mounted.

They rode another hour then stopped for lunch at a small Mexican restaurant that bordered their property at the highway. The lot was full of cars from all over, but Juan Carlos had never allowed the horse posts behind his restaurant to be removed.

The five began to dismount when a back door swung open—a short, slender man standing in the opening. "So you made it today, Heath," Juan Carlos called out.

"That we did. You got room for five?"

"Always, my friend." He greeted everyone and was introduced to Annie. She'd never eaten at his restaurant.

The food was good and plentiful. A new basket of hot chips with salsa appeared just as the old basket was nearly empty. Annie was silent most of the time, listening to the MacLarens discuss ranch business, a new townhome project Heath had going, and Cassie's new boyfriend. The last kept the conversation going for much of the time. She and Seth Garner's grandson had gone out a couple of times, which was news to Heath.

They'd known Matt Garner his whole life. He was a year older than Cassie, attended a local community college, and worked in his grandfather's construction company—a company that did a lot of business with the MacLarens. Matt's parents had been close friends of Heath and his first wife, Pamela, until they'd been killed in a small plane crash when Matt was ten. Their grandfather, Seth Garner, had raised him, along with his younger brother, Troy, on his small ranch that bordered the MacLarens on one side.

"I never realized you had any interest at all in Matt." Caroline put the last bite of an enchilada in her mouth and sat back, interested in this new development.

"Neither did I until he asked me to a party a few weeks ago. Besides, he was always with Becky Fraser during high school. She went off to college in another state, he stayed here, and well," Cassie paused a moment, "I guess we both discovered how much we enjoyed being around each other." She threw her napkin on the table. "Are we ready to ride back yet?"

"Guess we are." Heath thanked Juan Carlos before heading outside. He looked around at the darkening sky. "Looks like we'd better ride straight back, Jace. Those clouds are moving pretty fast."

"I see them. Let's detour through the old gulch. That will get us home within an hour."

They didn't ride hard, just kept a steady pace without stopping. About halfway home Heath heard a sharp whinny, then another. He reined Blackjack around to see Gremlin buck a couple of times, Annie bring him under control for a brief moment before Gremlin bucked again, this time throwing her off. It was pure luck that Annie hadn't landed in a stand of small cacti a few feet away.

Gremlin took off but stopped a hundred yards away. Heath rode up to the frightened animal, grabbed the reins, and turned back to the others. Everyone else surrounded Annie, checking for breaks, then helping her stand.

Heath handed Gremlin's reins to Jace and slid off his horse. "You all right?"

"Yes, I'm fine. Something must have spooked him. He just started bucking. I thought I had him under control, but guess not." Annie grimaced at a sharp pain in her lower back.

"I'm calling the doc. Get him out to check on you." He pulled out his cell phone to dial.

"No, please don't. I'm fine, really. It feels more like bruising, no breaks."

"But..."

"No doctor, Heath. Please." Annie's distress at calling the doctor was more pronounced than the pain she felt from the spill.

He let out a sharp breath. "If that's what you want. But if you're still in pain when we get back to the house I'm calling the doctor. Period."

"Deal."

The group waited another ten minutes to let Annie walk around and stretch, while Jace and Heath checked on Gremlin.

"No bites that I can see. Looks like he may have a slight sprain. I don't think he should be ridden." Jace knew horses better than anyone else in the family. They were his passion. "I'll lead him if Annie can ride back with you."

"Sure." Heath let the women know. He helped Annie onto Blackjack then swung up behind her. "Let's go," he called.

He wrapped one arm around her waist, pulling her close, and held the reins in the other. Annie wasn't prepared for the way the solid wall of man made her feel. She sucked in a breath when they rode up a small hill that had her pushing closer into him.

"You all right?" Heath asked, enjoying the feel of her close to him and the smell of her hair. He

38

found himself breathing in her unique scent and had to concentrate to keep the hand around her waist instead of letting it wander, explore. He tightened his hold a little.

"Yes, fine." *Too fine.* "I just haven't ridden double in a long time."

"Won't be for long. Look around that bend ahead and you'll see the ranch house."

Thirty minutes later Heath dismounted and helped Annie down. "You okay because I have no issue with bringing the doctor out here or taking you to his office."

"I'm fine, truly. Besides, it's Saturday. He wouldn't be around anyway and I won't go to emergency."

"Oh, he'd come out here if I called." He watched her walk around another moment. "Are you sure you don't want me to call?"

"I am. I hope this won't stop you from inviting me again sometime. It was great."

"Hey, you did fine. To be honest, you handled yourself better than some of my wranglers. Gremlin's a good horse so it had to be a snake or something. You're welcome anytime." Heath turned abruptly at the sound of a car driving up to the house.

"Another, young hottie, Dad?" Cassie asked.

Heath's head snapped around at his daughter. "That's enough, Cassie. It's Laurel. I invited her out to look at a horse. She's thinking of buying one and taking riding lessons from Caroline."

"Yeah, right." Cassie glared at the young woman who stepped out of the sporty, red convertible, but masked her disgust with a thin smile. "I've got to clean up. Going to a movie with Matt tonight. Nice to meet you, Annie." She was gone before Heath had a chance to utter another word.

Laurel waved to him. He knew Cassie was right. Laurel was twenty-eight but looked much younger. She'd been carded at each of the places he'd taken her. At forty-five maybe he needed to be with someone who at least looked to be in her thirties.

"Goodbye, Heath. Thanks again." Annie strolled to her car, opened the back door, and threw in her gear. She glanced back to see Laurel place a quick kiss on Heath's lips, then move toward Jace and Caroline. She'd obviously met Heath's family before.

She was just starting the engine when Heath appeared at her window.

"Annie, come on out for supper tomorrow. My son is flying in later today. He'll be joining the board sometime after his commitment to the Navy is over. I'd like you to meet him. It will give Caroline, Jace, and I a chance to catch you up on some of our plans."

"If I won't be intruding on a family dinner then I'd be glad to come out."

"Good, we'll see you tomorrow." He shifted his gaze to Laurel. "Guess I'd better get back. Time to sell a woman a horse."

Annie noticed Heath's grin didn't quite reach his eyes and wondered if his life was truly as idyllic as she'd first thought.

Chapter Five

Before Annie knew it, spring had turned to early summer. She'd spent a lot of time at the MacLaren ranch, as well as going to baseball games in Phoenix, and various events around Fire Mountain. The spring softball league had started and they'd invited her to join their team. Heath had insisted it was strictly for fun, but with their competitive streak, anything the MacLarens did also included a certain amount of determination to come out ahead.

She'd played softball in high school and some in college but it had been years since she'd felt the leather conform to her hand. They put her in right field, then moved her to left, then second base over the first couple of months. Her fielding skills were better than her batting but at least she didn't embarrass herself too often.

"Annie!" Heath yelled and pointed in the air to a pop-up fly ball. It was between Heath, the pitcher, and her position at second base.

She kept her eye on the ball and trotted forward a few feet only to collide with a thud against an immovable wall. Heath. She lost her balance and fell backwards onto the ground.

"Hey, that was my ball," she laughed before grabbing the hand he offered.

"Didn't think you saw it," Heath grinned.

"You did get it, right?"

He held up his gloved hand with the ball tucked neatly inside.

"Okay, then the fall was worth it." Annie bent down to brush the dirt from her pants and turned to head back to her position.

"Where you going? That was third out. Game over. We won."

She looked back to see Jace, Cassie, and Matt standing together laughing. She shook her head and trotted towards them. Everyone headed to the dugout for their gear.

"All right, hamburgers or pizza tonight?" Caroline asked when they were all at their cars.

"Count us out," Cassie said. "A group of friends are meeting for Italian at Rossi's."

"Well, in that case I say we go for steak and ribs," Heath said and winked at Annie.

"Dad, that's not right," Cassie tossed back, turning to stand in front of him.

"Hey, all's fair when we're talking food. You're welcome to join us or go for spaghetti."

Matt walked up and put an arm around Cassie. "I say steak and ribs, then go to Rossi's for tiramisu." He smiled at Heath over the top of Cassie's head.

Steak, ribs, and tiramisu won.

Three nights later Caroline, Jace, and Annie met for the release of a new action movie. The lights were dimmed and the previews had just finished when Annie noticed someone had taken the seat next to her.

"What are you doing here?" she asked Heath who was settling into his seat.

"Changed my mind. Decided the movie sounded better than what I'd had planned." He sat back and grabbed a handful of popcorn from the tub in Annie's lap.

"Hey," Annie slapped at his hand. "Get your own."

"What and miss the first part of the movie?" He reached in for another handful and stuffed it into his mouth. "I'll get you a refill if you need it," he smiled and leaned back to watch the film.

The summer continued to pass. Annie and Heath had settled into an easy friendship, spending considerable time together, sometimes seeing each other several times a week. They'd become what Caroline called buddies without benefits. Annie thought that was an apt description. If Heath didn't have a date for something, he called Annie. If she needed a date, she called Heath. Most times he was available, sometimes not, but it was a good arrangement.

Most important, they'd each found they could talk candidly with each other about almost any subject. Heath confided in Annie about his failed marriage that he'd stayed in until his ex-wife had confessed to having an affair with a professional ball player who'd retired to Scottsdale. Truth was, he was relieved. There'd been no love between them for years, more of an ongoing tolerance for the sake of Trey and Cassie.

Annie talked about her discomfort of being anywhere near a hospital or doctor. She'd spent uncounted hours and days during Kit's illness in medical facilities in Fire Mountain, Phoenix, and Los Angeles trying to find the magic cure. Of course, there wasn't one.

Annie had just stepped outside the grocery when her cell rang.

"Hey, Annie, it's Heath."

She knew that—his name came up on the phone. "Hi, Heath."

"Look, I need to head to Denver for a meeting on the Friday before the fourth. I was going to take Cassie and Matt to the rodeo that night. Would you be able to take my place?"

"Sure, I'd love to. Did you want to give away our tickets for Sunday?" They were supposed to go with Jace and Caroline to the Sunday night rodeo after a BBQ at the ranch.

"Hell, no. I want to go, just can't make it on Friday."

"No problem, you're covered."

"Thanks. I owe you." He hung up without another word. Annie stared at the dead call smiling at how natural they were together.

She'd found herself hoping that he kept dating women too young and too self-centered to be interested in a relationship or anything permanent. This had turned into one of the best summers she'd had in a long time. One summer was spent with Kit's illness, and two more sitting alone, trying to build a desire to forge a new life. This year, with Heath, she'd done more in a few short months than she'd done in the previous three years. His friendship was just what she needed to find herself again and look toward the future.

Annie and the kids had a great time at the rodeo. She knew Heath liked Matt, a lot, although he didn't think either he or Cassie were old enough to make it a permanent thing. Besides, Cassie was heading to ASU in two months while Matt was staying at the local college one more year. They'd probably both move on once that happened.

"What are you up to the rest of the weekend, besides the BBQ on Sunday?" Annie asked as the barrel-racing event continued. She'd been told this was the first year Cassie hadn't competed in the event since she'd first qualified.

"We're going to visit friends in Clayton then having dinner with my grandpa tomorrow," Matt said. Clayton was a small town about an hour northwest of Fire Mountain.

"What are you doing, Annie. You dating anyone?" Cassie asked at the same time Matt wrapped his hand around hers.

"Not really. I've had dinner a couple of times with someone, but I don't know. It just doesn't feel quite right."

"Who?" Cassie persisted.

"That is something I'll tell you if it turns into something more." She smiled at the younger woman.

"You and Dad should date, not just do this buddy stuff."

Annie was surprised by the comment. Cassie knew as well as anyone that Annie wasn't Heath's type—never would be. "Your father and I are fine just the way we are. He's a good friend but that's all it will ever be." She returned her gaze to the ring as the final barrel racer started her course.

The two young people heard the sorrow in her voice and wondered if she realized how much that revealed about her feelings toward Heath.

Cassie reached into her pocket, touching the answer mode as she brought the phone to her ear. "Hi, Dad. Yeah, we're here." She listened a while to Heath. "Sounds good. Yes. I'll ask her. See you tomorrow evening." She closed the call and slipped the phone back in her pocket. "The meeting is going well, he'll be home tomorrow afternoon. Said to ask you if you had any plans for dinner tomorrow night, Annie. He wants to talk to you about something regarding the foundation. He'll call you later tonight."

The rodeo concluded and Annie headed back to her place. She was behind schedule on one of her books and needed to get something out by the following Friday.

The impact of driving onto the one-acre lot never diminished for Annie. She loved the house, the location, and the way she now felt complete peace when she walked inside. It hadn't been that way a few months ago. At that time it was more of a refuge, a place to hide from the world. Now it was a welcome sight.

Annie dropped her purse on the counter, made some tea, and walked down the hall to her small office that looked out toward the front yard. Most of her work was done in this room. Once in a while she'd unplug her laptop and take it into the bedroom or family room, or even the back deck, but that was rare. She activated her computer screen then reached over and turned on some music. She'd work a couple of hours, check email, and go to bed. Tomorrow she hoped to finish the bulk of her newest novel and get in a workout before getting ready for dinner with Heath.

It was unusual that he didn't have a date on a Saturday night. Who was it he'd been seeing lately? Julia, that was her name. He'd met her in early May, brought her to the Memorial Weekend shindig at the ranch. A couple of weeks ago Heath had told Annie that Julia had moved to California. He was glad as it made things easier. Heath wasn't ready for anything more.

It was fine with Annie, too. She knew that the minute Heath ever told her he'd met someone special that their relationship would change. Few women accepted a female friend with ease. Besides, maybe some distance from Heath would encourage other men to ask her out. It was time to find a life away from the MacLarens and one in particular.

When that time came, Annie would back away, flow out of his life the way she'd flowed into it. It would be the best for all.

Chapter Six

Annie was exhausted. It was late-August and she'd gone with the MacLarens to a private camp ground hours northeast of Fire Mountain. It was a magnificent area with a beautiful river, lake, and tall mountains. They'd stayed four nights and five days, fishing and riding their horses through the vast wilderness area. Their land butted against a huge national forest, making for the perfect private playground.

They'd just finished a day of riding and fishing, hauling their catch by horseback to the camp site. It was their last night before driving back in the morning.

"Here, give those to me," Heath said and took the string of trout from Annie's hand. He, Jace, Matt, and Jace's boys, Blake and Brett, set to work cleaning the fish while the women prepared the rest of the meal.

The meal had been a feast. Now they all relaxed around the campfire, roasting marshmallows, then placing them between graham crackers and chocolate. Nothing was better when camping and s'mores.

"What's the plan for Labor Day, Dad?" Cassie sat next to Matt, stuffing another s'more in her mouth.

"Same as always. We'll ride in the parade on Saturday, Frontier Day picnic on Sunday, then have a BBQ at the ranch on Monday. Unless anyone has a better idea." Heath grabbed another beer and tossed one to Jace.

"Sounds good to me," Jace said and caught the beer.

"Same here. Why change a good thing?" Caroline drank her soda and watched the setting sun.

"Annie? You want to ride in the parade with us?" Heath asked.

"I don't have a trailer for Rascal. Maybe I'll just watch."

"That's not what I asked. Do you want to ride with us?" Heath asked again.

"Why, yes. It would be fun."

"Fine. Then I can pick up Rascal and bring him over with our horses, or you can ride Gremlin. Your choice."

She hated for him to go to extra work. Besides, she'd ridden Gremlin several times over the summer including the last four days. He was used to riding around other horses, which Rascal wasn't. "I'll ride Gremlin." She smiled and looked towards the horses.

"Gremlin it is. We'll meet you at the staging area at seven o'clock. Parade starts at nine." Heath grabbed another s'more and handed it to Annie, then sat down beside her. Their heads were close as Heath spoke quietly. Both laughed.

Jace slipped an arm around his wife. "You think they have any idea of what's happening between them?" he asked.

"Not a clue," Caroline responded.

"I think Heath's finally hooked, he just doesn't know it."

"You know, even if he figures it out, he may not acknowledge it."

"Yeah, I know." Jace took a swallow of beer and set down his can. "Nothing we can do but watch it play out."

"I just worry about Annie, that's all."

"Understood, but they're adults. They'll have to figure this out on their own." Jace pulled her a little closer and pressed a kiss on her cheek, knowing how blessed he was to still have Caroline in his life.

******

"Okay everyone, line up as we discussed," Heath shouted to the assembled riders. They were one of the first groups to go. The MacLarens had participated in the parade every year since its inception.

There were twelve in four rows of three riders each. Heath, Jace, and Matt took the lead row with the others spaced out behind them. Most were MacLarens plus some close friends who'd ridden in the parade every year with them for a long time. Annie was the newbie, so they'd put her in the middle.

Like many towns, Fire Mountain's Labor Day weekend parade included every civic group, school, non-profit, and major employer for miles. Groups representing the fire fighters, police, and sheriff, as well as elected officials all had a spot. School bands were located throughout the long line of participants including a few from smaller towns that couldn't support a parade.

Annie heard the music at the same time she saw Heath turn towards her and smile.

"You okay, Annie?"

"Great, Heath. This is exciting, don't you think?" A smile lit her face.

"Yeah, Annie, it is." Heath watched her a moment then turned back to the front.

She'd become very important to him over the last months. Whenever he had a problem, he called Annie—even before Jace. She was a good listener and offered input only when asked. And he knew she expected nothing from him.

They'd had more fun the last few months than he'd had in years. She enjoyed everything that he did. Heath thought of the first time she'd ridden on the back of his Harley. Her worry had turned to laughs as they traveled the county's back roads. She'd gone out the next day and bought special boots, jacket, and gloves. He'd presented her with a custom painted helmet with her name. They'd ridden almost every week since and planned to ride after the parade today then go to dinner.

The parade moved along. Heath took a deep breath and nudged Blackjack a little to keep up the pace. He had a new possible business deal in

Phoenix. It had come to his attention during his trip to Denver just before July fourth. The company he was working with on a new retail center in Denver was interested in the same type of venture in north Phoenix.

They'd hired a new director in charge of the retail group for Phoenix. She was bright, someone he thought he could work well with, and didn't hurt that she was a knock-out. Later this weekend he'd pencil out some ideas. If it made sense he'd call her Tuesday for a meeting.

******

"Faster Annie or they'll pass us," Heath urged. It was the Saturday before Halloween and the town had planned a picnic and fund-raiser for the local fire fighters. Annie and Heath had paired up for the three-legged race. It was a usual part of most picnics in Fire Mountain. They were in the lead, but only because Heath hated to lose. She'd never met anyone so competitive.

"I'm going as fast as I can," she laughed and almost fell to the side.

Heath wrapped an arm around her to stop the momentum. Six yards, four yards. "We're almost there."

Three more surges and they'd crossed the line first. Both collapsed and fell into fits of laughter. "I don't think it has ever been that close," Heath said between deep breaths. "I need a beer." He reached down to start untying their legs, brushing against her skin, causing a warm sensation to move up her body. It was like this anytime they touched, like electric currents moving from one end of her body to the other. He may not notice it but she sure did.

Annie reached down and shoved his hands away. "I'll do it." She had the ties loosened in a few seconds. "Guess I'll go get a drink, too."

Heath watched her walk away. The last two days had been good, just like every day since Annie and he had become friends. They'd laughed, talked, and gotten along just like always, as if there wasn't something weighing on him.

For the first time, he had doubts about what he was doing. It had all seemed so clear. Now, he wasn't sure. Annie had become so important to him, essential to his sanity. What if everything changed and she pushed him away? He understood that a man never knew what a woman would do. Did that include Annie? In a few short months she'd become a close friend, a confidante, as crucial as the air he breathed.

"Here you go," Annie handed him a cold beer.

He took it and popped the top. "Thanks." Heath watched her gulp down the diet soda she held, enjoying the sight of the joy he saw. She swallowed and smiled down at him.

"That was great. Thanks for asking me to partner up."

"You can be my partner anytime, Annie." The words had just come out. Now Heath wished he could take them back because he knew they weren't true. He liked her much more than he'd ever intended, loved her as a friend, except at some point he knew things were bound to change—

perhaps soon. Everything changed, especially relationships that had once been special.

"Okay, you two. It's time for Dad to help the other men with the barbeque. Everything else is ready." Cassie had driven home from ASU for the event. She ran up and reached a hand out to her father. "You need help up, old man?" she teased.

"I'll show you old," he said and pulled her down to him. Cassie giggled when Heath started to tickle her. "You need to show me some respect, young lady. Do you give?"

"Never!" Cassie yelled.

"Okay, then." Heath tickled again and watched her erupt into more laughter.

"All right! I give!"

He let her go and rolled to his side before hoisting himself up. "Right decision," he said and reached a hand to his daughter. "Come on you two, let's get this food thing going."

******

"You want anything more, Dad," Cassie asked as she walked around with a platter of steak and burgers. "This is all that's left. If you want it, better grab it now."

"Nope, honey, I'm full. You'll have to pawn it off on the others." Heath lay back on the reclining chair positioned to watch all the happenings. He checked his watch. Five o'clock. It was time to get Annie home.

Heath walked around the expansive park, checking each group for Annie, then he heard her laugh. It was distinctive, the type you'd recognize out of a large crowd. He turned to see her speaking with Seth Garner and his date. Annie was a picture—long light blond hair, emerald green top over white capris, and white sandals. Seth said something and she laughed again, causing Seth's date to smile.

Annie turned her smile toward Heath, and if possible, it brightened even more. The effect hit him in his gut causing him to stop mid-stride. He shoved his hands in his pants pockets and looked down at the ground. When he looked up Annie stood before him.

"You all right?" she asked, watching him with concern in her eyes.

Heath cleared his throat. "Uh, yeah, fine. I was just looking for you. Thought you might be ready to leave."

"Oh, that's right. I'd forgotten you'd picked me up. Just let me grab my sweater." She dashed to where they'd left their things and was back within a minute. "Caroline boxed up all my stuff in her car. Okay if I come to the ranch tomorrow to grab my plates and silverware?"

"Sure, Annie, whatever you want."

She said her goodbyes and met Heath at his truck a few minutes later. "If you have someplace to go, I can ask Cassie or Caroline to give me a ride."

"No problem. Hop in." Heath started the engine as soon as she'd shut her door.

It took just a few minutes to get from the park to her front door. The late afternoon sun was just touching the peaks of the western slopes. Clouds hung above hinting that there'd be a brilliant sunset. That's one of the things Annie liked best—the striking deep red and yellow sunsets over the mountains. She never tired of the sight.

"Do you have a few minutes to come inside?" Annie asked.

"Sure. I could use some coffee for the trip."

She unlocked the front door and stepped in, Heath right behind her. "Trip?"

"Yes, I, uh, need to drive to Phoenix tonight for another meeting tomorrow."

"On Sunday?"

"Unfortunately, that's when the retail marketing director is available." It wasn't a lie yet wasn't the truth. The half-truth felt wrong.

Annie made him a cup of coffee and set it before him and grabbed one for herself, adding the milk and sweetener she favored.

He sipped slowly, watching her over the rim of his cup.

"Oh, I almost forgot." Annie walked around the counter, opened a cabinet, and pulled out a pie pan. "I have a surprise for you." She pulled off the cover to reveal a berry pie, Heath's favorite. "I think I may have gotten it right this time." Annie tilted it up for him to see.

"That looks wonderful, Annie."

"How big a slice?" She pulled open a drawer and picked up a serving knife.

"I've met someone," Heath said in a low, soft voice.

"Oh, yeah, who?" She continued to busy herself pulling down plates.

"No, I mean I've met someone, Annie."

As if struck by a dart, his meaning pierced her consciousness, and just that quick, her heart. She set down the plates and dropped her hands to her sides.

"You mean a woman?"

"Yes."

"Well, that's, uh, great, Heath. Really, wonderful." She fought for breath as her chest constricted. He'd never spoken this way about anyone he'd dated. They were just dates. This was specific and, in her mind, brought finality to their idyllic friendship.

"She lives in Phoenix. I'm seeing her when I get to the city." He set his coffee cup down and focused on Annie. She had said the right things, was smiling. Then why did something seem so wrong?

In an instant he realized what it was. Her bright smile was fixed, as if frozen in time. The light in her eyes had dimmed, like a chandelier whose brilliance darkened with the twist of a switch.

"It sounds like you've been seeing her for a while then." It was a statement, not an accusation or a question. The impact of the situation hit her full force, and Annie realized, for the first time, that she'd fallen in love with this man—a man who would never return her feelings. The same man she'd sworn to herself would never mean more to her than that of a friend. She'd lied to herself long enough.

He watched her, already knowing he'd made a mistake bringing it up this way. "A few weeks. You'd like her, Annie. She is truly something. I'd like to introduce you when she has time to get away. Maybe next weekend."

Meet her? She'd just realized she was in love with him and he was talking about introducing her to the woman who now meant a great deal to him.

She ignored his comment, forging ahead with the mental groundwork she'd set in place. "Of course. Whatever works for the two of you." She pretended to check the time. "Guess you'd better get going. The traffic will be miserable—you know what it's like on the southbound freeway some days. I'll just wrap this up, you can take it with you, because I'll certainly never eat it." She reached for the foil, tore a piece, and covered the pie. "There, perfect for traveling. I hope she likes berry. But..." she was rambling, making no sense. Why couldn't he just leave?

"Annie..."

"Here you go." She smiled her too bright, too fixed smile, handed him the pie then walked past him to the door and pulled it open. "Still plenty of light for at least part of the drive." She stood with her hand on the knob, unable to move, waiting for him to pass by.

Heath looked at the pie, stared at it in his hands, wanting to put it back on the counter, and explain. If he could just tell her about Diana, Annie would understand. She was just surprised, that's all. She hadn't expected him to blurt this out. He'd caught her off guard. Heath took a long breath and raised his head. Annie stood at the door, waiting for him to leave.

He stepped to the door and bent to place a quick kiss on her cheek. "I'll call you when I get back in a few days. We can meet for lunch."

"Sure, whatever you want." Annie knew she'd find an excuse to not see him. She needed to be upfront with him. "Look, Heath. I'd love to meet your special woman, and I am happy for you, honestly. But I'm sure she wouldn't be thrilled knowing you have a female buddy. Women are funny that way. It'd be best if you concentrated on her for a while. There will be plenty of time for me to meet her. Besides, I need to get back to all the things I've put off."

He stared at her. "Such as?"

"Well, I have several book projects, publicity and marketing, cover design work..." Her voice trailed off and faded completely.

"Annie, just let me tell you about her." Heath started to walk back in, but Annie put a hand to his chest, then removed it as if it was a flaming torch that would burn her if she lingered too long.

"Not tonight. I'm sure she's an amazing woman. You can explain everything to me some other time when you don't have a long drive ahead of you."

He felt his throat work but couldn't find any words he knew would change her mind or let him demolish the wall she'd built between them within a matter of minutes. A friendship he cherished was crumbling before his eyes. "All right. But I'll see you Saturday night at Caroline's for dinner. You do remember she's having a dinner party and you're my date?"

"It would be best if you asked Diana to come up from Phoenix. Seems like the perfect time to introduce her to your family. Unless they've already met her." Annie stopped to wonder if she was the last one to learn about Diana. "Besides, I meant to tell you and Caroline, I have other plans that night." She had no doubt he knew the lie the moment it crossed her lips. It didn't matter. Her days of being his buddy were in the past. He'd moved on and now it was up to her to do the same.

"If that's what you want."

"Yes, it is."

He reached for her wanting to pull her into his arms. She backed away.

"Drive carefully. Wouldn't want you to slam on the breaks and splatter the pie all over your leather seats." She tried to make it a joke without success.

"Well, goodnight, then. I'll talk with you soon." He turned toward his car and heard the door close and the click of a lock sliding into place. He felt as if she'd closed him out of her house and her life in the span of a few wrenching heartbeats.

Chapter Seven

He drove without the radio, clutching the steering wheel, and peering into oncoming headlights that almost blinded him. The traffic was as bad as Annie had projected, maybe worse. He knew his disposition was.

Heath played over their conversation so many times that he couldn't think any longer. Every word was burned into his mind, and still it made no sense. She said she was happy for him. Thrilled that he'd found someone. Yet the way she'd pushed him to leave, wouldn't let him tell about Diana told a different story.

Was she right that Diana wouldn't understand his bond with Annie? How she'd been the one to listen to his long ramblings after finishing a bottle of Jameson, not one night, but several? She'd listened, made coffee, helped him to bed, and then curled up in one of the guest rooms, ready to help him with his raging hangover the next morning.

Would any woman understand the depth of the friendship Annie and he shared?

They'd talked of his failed marriage, his inability to love his wife, and his fear that he'd never be able to feel the things that came naturally to most men. She understood his need to date younger women who would never be a real part of his life. Not like Annie, who was more real to him than any woman he'd known—until now.

He thought he had a chance with Diana. He didn't love her, hadn't connected with her like Annie, but he felt in time he could. Diana was bright, exciting, passionate about her work, and one of the most beautiful women he'd ever known. The sex was nothing short of amazing even if it lacked the depth of feeling he so desperately wanted to find.

Maybe Annie was right that his friendship with her would interfere with his desire to build a relationship with Diana. Perhaps she was right to back away and he was wrong to expect Diana to simply accept his deep friendship with another woman.

Heath pounded the steering wheel then gripped it tighter. He'd figure something out. Their friendship was as important to Annie as it was to him—it was a fact he'd stake his life on. He'd just have to find a way to keep his friendship with her intact while he built a relationship with Diana.

******

Annie woke to a blinding headache. She rubbed her eyes, pushing in on her temples, seeking relief from the incessant pounding. It had been a mistake to drink the last of the scotch, then start on the bottle of Jameson she kept for Heath.

Heath.

She closed her eyes and let the pain settle in again. At least the alcohol had deadened it somewhat. Now it emerged fiercer than ever. Her rational mind told her that the ache would subside a little each day until it disappeared or at least became bearable.

It had been a mistake to let him into her life, let him be the friend she'd lost when Kit died. She should have stuck with her girlfriends, ignoring Heath, and his insistent invitations.

The thing was, they'd meshed so well, as if they'd know each other forever. They fell into long discussions and confided things they'd never told anyone else. When she thought about it, the whole friendship, so quick and seemingly so strong, was destined to burn out in time. The minute the right woman came along, their friendship would be a hindrance. Perhaps he didn't understand it now, but Annie knew it for the truth it was. Women did not tolerate female best buddies. It just didn't happen.

Annie heard her cell phone and reached a hand out to her nightstand. Nothing. She must have left it in her purse, which was still in the kitchen. She didn't feel like rushing to pick it up and let it go to voice mail.

Annie walked to the bathroom, brushed her teeth, and turned on the shower. Showers always helped. There was something about hot water rushing over her body that allowed her to shut out the world, if only for a brief period. Annie grabbed the body scrubber, squeezed on some wash, and ran it over her body. Lightly at first, then harder, then harder still. The hot water stung her skin where she'd scrubbed.

An image drifted across her mind as the hot water sluiced down her body. It was of Heath, his naked back to her. When he lifted his head and looked behind him, Annie saw someone beneath him. A stunning woman, naked, with her arms wrapped around his neck. Annie's chest tightened and a hand came up to push at the pain. As she worked to control the hurt and rid herself of the image, an agonized sob escaped, then another until her body shook. She slid to the floor and sobbed until there was nothing left and the intense ache subsided.

Annie had no idea how long she'd sat under the water. She reached up and turned it off, wrapped towels around her long hair and body, stepped out of the shower then sat down on a small bench, leaning her back against the wall and closing her eyes.

It was Sunday, a day she dedicated to writing if she had no other plans. The best way to move on was to get back into her routine. Dress, make coffee, check emails, and write. It didn't matter which unfinished story she worked on as long it was something that consumed her thoughts.

She sat for two hours, staring at the screen, occasionally tapping away on her keyboard as snippets of the story came to life. For that span of time she worked to clear her mind of Heath and his new romance. She began to feel somewhat better. Later, she'd workout, maybe grab a sandwich at the little shop she liked, check her mail box, then write some more.

It was a day to start over.

******

Heath checked his watch. Eleven-thirty on Monday. He'd spent Saturday night and Sunday with Diana. More uninterrupted time with her than any woman he'd known after his divorce, except Annie. Heath was bewildered. He'd spent most of the time thinking about Annie and their friendship than about the woman in his bed. It wasn't what he'd expected.

He was taking Diana to lunch down the street from her office. The meeting that morning had gone well, now all that held up the deal was the drafting of a final agreement with the modifications that all approved. He'd sign the papers this afternoon then celebrate. Perhaps he'd take Diana to the fancy restaurant they both liked, the one he'd taken her to on their first date several weeks ago.

"Hi. You ready?" Diana stood before him, dressed in a stunning steel gray suit with a short skirt, peach colored blouse, and high heels. She was twelve years younger, thirty-one, with jet black hair that dropped to her shoulders, minimal makeup, and soft grey-green eyes.

"All ready. Where to?"

"Just down the street to Baker's. It's quiet, we can get a small table near the back." She placed a slim hand in his. "I have no appointments until the meeting to sign the agreement this afternoon at five o'clock. We may have to find some way to fill our time." Her suggestive smile wasn't lost on Heath, so why didn't it tempt him?

They walked to the restaurant in silence. The normal small talk could wait until they were seated. For some reason Heath was edgy, couldn't seem to clear his head and relax. It had been that way since his conversation, or lack of one, with Annie.

His first thought after the hand-shake this morning, sealing the proposed deal, was to call Annie. He'd worked three months on the final aspects of the partnership to expand a center that MacLaren Properties owned in north Phoenix. Long nights, weekly trips to the city, unending phone conferences, and hard negotiations had finally paid off.

He'd grabbed the phone from his pocket and began to punch her number, then stopped. The realization that Annie might not pick up the call, wouldn't be the first to congratulate him, be excited for his accomplishment, twisted something in his chest. It was as if a vise gripped him and squeezed. It made no sense. They were good friends, nothing more. Why did he feel this acute sense of loss?

"I'll have a glass of white wine, Peter," Heath heard Diana tell the waiter.

"Jameson, on the rocks."

"I'll get your drinks then take your order," the waiter said and left them alone.

"How does it feel to finally settle a deal you've worked so hard to win?" Diana asked with a gleam in her eyes.

"Good." Not great, just good.

"So, what's next on your agenda? Other deals in Phoenix or somewhere else?"

"Nothing specific. I have a few vague ideas but they need to be fleshed out a little more to see if they make sense."

"Here you are, one white wine, and your whiskey, sir." The drinks were placed before them.

They ordered and picked up their glasses.

"To your success today, Heath," Diana toasted.

They touched glasses, Diana taking a small sip, Heath drinking half of his amber liquid. Somehow he didn't feel like a success.

******

"We're looking forward to this partnership, Heath. Will you be available sometime next week to go over the drawings and review the numbers?" Tom Elliott was the senior partner he'd worked with over the last three months. Diana worked for Tom and was on the fast-track from what Heath had heard.

"Next week is fine, Tom. Let me know when and I'll make myself available."

"You heading north tonight or staying over?"

Heath glanced at Diana. She'd been less than thrilled when he'd told her he needed to return to Fire Mountain that evening. He still could change his mind, but he felt the need to return, finish his conversation with Annie.

"I'll be driving back this evening. I'm taking Diana to dinner, would you care to join us?" A sharp look from Diana warned him he'd made another error.

"I'd like to but I have other plans. Count me in for next week."

The men shook hands and Heath walked out, signed agreement in hand, with Diana following a few steps behind.

"Diana," Tom called. "Do you have a moment?"

"Of course." She looked at Heath. "I'll meet you in the lobby."

"That's fine. I have some calls I need to make."

He settled into a large, leather chair in the reception area and dialed Annie's number. No answer. He left a short message, letting her know his deal had gone through and asking if her schedule had any openings. After two more calls he slid the phone into his pocket and waited. Thirty minutes passed before Diana came around the corner. She walked up and stood before him.

"What's that smile about?" Heath asked.

"Tom gave me some pretty exciting news. I'll tell you over dinner."

They drove his car to a small Italian restaurant on the way to her townhome in Scottsdale. They had ridden in together that morning. After dinner he'd drop Diana off at her place then head north toward home. He was ready to get back.

They were shown to their table, ordered, then Heath waited for Diana's big news.

"The reason Tom wanted to speak with me was to say the board was pleased with the way the negotiations went with MacLaren Properties." Excitement poured from her as she spoke.

"That's wonderful. Does it mean a promotion?"

"No, nothing like that yet, but at least I've had a chance to show them a little of what I can do. Perhaps if I continue like this I'll be offered my own office and staff."

"How many offices does the company have?"

"Twelve across the country. One in each of their major target areas."

"So a promotion would mean a move outside of Arizona. When it comes, it will be a big decision." He sipped the Jameson, not at all sure what this meant as far as trying to build something with her, but it was too soon to turn his back on this yet. A promotion might not come for months, or years, if at all.

They made small talk through dinner, passing on dessert. When the check came she grabbed it. "This one's on me, Heath."

They drove in silence to her place. He opened the door of her townhome and stood aside so Diana could pass in front of him. Heath closed the door and turned to see that Diana had already removed her jacket and was unbuttoning her blouse while moving towards him. In an instant he knew this wasn't what he wanted, at least not tonight.

"How long do we have before you need to leave?" Her voice was low, seductive. She opened the front of her blouse and let it fall to the floor. Next she unclasped the front of her bra. It followed her blouse. She reached behind her drawing the zipper to her skirt down and letting it pool at her feet. She stood before him, all legs and black lace panties, tempting him.

He watched her, getting hard despite his efforts to stay in control. She took two steps, stopping inches from his chest. "See anything that makes you want to stay for a while?" She splayed her hands on his chest before undoing the top button of his shirt, then the next button, and the next. She pulled it open to reveal course, dark hair, then leaned forward to place kisses on his chest.

He leaned back against the door and took a deep breath. Her hands had moved to his pants. He felt a button release and heard the rasping of a zipper.

Heath placed a hand under her chin lifting her face to his. He lowered his mouth to hers and took control, plundering, and driving them both to the edge before lifting her into his arms.

An hour later he lay in her bed, feeling sated yet hollow. She had everything he thought he wanted, yet offered nothing he needed. He rolled off the bed, dressed, and grabbed his keys. Bending down he placed a kiss on her cheek.

"I'll call you," he whispered.

"Hmmm. Make it soon." Diana's sleepy voice followed him as he left for the drive to Fire Mountain.

Chapter Eight

"Have you heard from her?" Jace asked the Saturday after Heath had returned from Phoenix.

"Nope." Heath concentrated on the paperwork in front of him.

"Did you leave her a message about the board meeting?"

"I did. I'm sure she'll be there. Annie told me last weekend that she had several deadlines and wouldn't be available much this week."

"And dinner tonight at our place? Caroline mentioned that Annie's coming."

Heath looked up. "Has she spoken with Annie this week?"

"Don't know, why?" Jace strolled over to a sideboard and filled his coffee cup.

Heath walked over to join his brother and top off his own cup. "She mentioned she couldn't make the dinner. Something had come up."

"Well, I'll leave that between the two of them. Caroline's buried with so many projects right now that she'll snap my head off if I bring up one more thing."

Heath chuckled at the thought of Caroline in a huff. She had more energy than three women and a sweet disposition, except when she committed herself to too much—which she often did.

"If we're done here I have that new colt to work. He's a smart one. You ought to come check him out when you have time." Jace walked to the office door and pulled it open. "You bringing someone tonight?"

"No, I'm coming solo."

Jace nodded. Something was up but he didn't have time right now to push his brother. "All right. See you later."

Heath watched Jace close the door. He tossed the pen on the stack of papers he'd been studying and wondered if he'd ever find a relationship like Jace and Caroline's. He thought back on eight years ago and the hell Jace had put Caroline through. No one believed their marriage would survive, but it did, and now they were the strongest couple he knew. Heath envied them.

He looked at the cell phone in front of him. After three messages and no return call he was hesitant to try again. Annie would get back to him. She wasn't ignoring him, just busy.

The ringing of his desk phone brought Heath back to his work.

"MacLaren," he said into the phone.

"What do you mean she's not coming?" He could hear the frustration in Caroline's voice. It was obvious Jace had rethought his previous decision and mentioned that Annie had bowed out of dinner.

"Hasn't she called you?" Heath asked.

"Not a word. I've left her a couple of messages but haven't heard back." Caroline paused. He could hear her soft breathing on the other end. "What's going on, Heath?"

Heath didn't want to talk about Annie with Caroline. "Don't know. She hasn't returned my calls either."

"Well, maybe you should go over there, make sure she's all right."

Heath had thought the same thing, then discarded the idea.

"I don't have the time today. If no one hears from her by Monday I'll stop by, make sure she's all right." Before Diana, he would have already been in his car.

The silence on the other end told Heath just what Caroline thought of his comment.

"I see."

"You see what?"

"Something is going on between you two but you're not ready to talk about it, right?"

"Look, Caroline. I appreciate your concern but there's nothing going on. We're both just busy." He loved his sister-in-law, and normally he might even mention his conversation with Annie, tell her about Diana, but not today. "I need to get back to my work. I'll see you and Jace tonight."

He hung up knowing that his evasive answer would only fuel Caroline's suspicions. She was one of the most intuitive people he knew.

Heath had spent the last few days reconsidering his eagerness to leave Diana Monday night. He'd overreacted, he was certain. Theirs was a new relationship and it would take time to build anything meaningful. He'd decided to continue seeing her, give them a chance.

He'd come to the conclusion he'd have to tell Jace and Caroline about Diana. Even though he wasn't certain of their future it might be wise to schedule something so Jace and Caroline could meet her. Heath was certain everyone would love her. Like they did Annie.

******

Caroline dialed Annie's number once more, hoping she'd pick up. If not, she'd feel compelled to drive over, make sure her friend was all right. One ring turned to five before Annie's voice mail picked up.

"Annie, this is Caroline. Where the heck are you? I've left two other messages. Call me." She hung up and slipped the phone back into her purse, grabbed the car keys, and dashed out the back door. Caroline was worried. Busy was one thing, but Annie had never stayed silent for this long.

Twenty minutes later she stood outside her friend's door. Caroline could see Annie's SUV through the garage window, knew she was inside.

She could hear movement inside and heard the lock slide back.

"Hi, Annie. What's going on?"

Annie was dressed in sweats, her hair in a ponytail, and a ten pound weight in one hand. "I don't know what you mean."

"Please. We've been friends long enough that I can tell when something isn't right. May I come in?"

Annie pulled the door open all the way knowing it was pointless to avoid this conversation any longer.

"You want something to drink? Soda, water, tequila?"

"Nothing. I just want to know what's going on. Are you upset with me? Did I do something?" The distress in Caroline's voice made Annie realize how selfish she'd been by not returning her calls.

"God, no. You've done nothing."

"Then what is it? I know you're busy, but you've never just shut me out."

Annie paced a few feet away then plopped down onto her sofa, letting out a deep breath, but didn't respond.

Caroline sat beside her and placed a hand on Annie's knee. "What is it? Let me help."

Annie leaned forward, placing her elbows on her knees, and covering her face with both hands.

"It's Heath." Annie dropped her hands and looked at Caroline. "He's met someone. A woman in Phoenix. It sounds serious."

Caroline fell back against the sofa. She'd known Annie had feelings for Heath. Now she realized that the feelings were much deeper than she'd thought.

"Did he tell you that?"

"When he brought me home from the picnic last Saturday he told me he'd met someone. Her name's Diana." She felt her chest squeeze but pushed the pain aside. "He's never done that before. Normally he just says he has a date and leaves it at that. This is the first time he's made it sound as if he's met someone special, a woman he wants to build a relationship with." Annie stopped, her gaze moving to the tall pines in the back yard. "I think he may be in love." She walked into the kitchen and stood by the counter.

The pain Caroline saw surprised her. She had no idea the extent of Annie's feelings for Heath. "So he may be in love with this Diana woman, and you're in love with him, right?"

"How did I let this happen? How could I have been so stupid? I'm a grown woman, with grown children. This wasn't supposed to be more than a friendship. How could I be so blind?" She slapped both hands on the counter and hung her head.

Caroline walked over and touched a hand to hers. "This isn't something within our control, honey. Never has been. You can't direct your heart to love or not love, it just doesn't work that way."

Annie glanced up, a tear making its way down her cheek. She swiped at it in frustration and at her total ignorance of her true feelings. "What am I supposed to do? He thinks we can carry on just like before, as close friends. He wants me to meet her. Oh, God, Caroline, I don't think I can do it."

Caroline squeezed her hand then stepped back. "You're a strong woman, Annie, one of the strongest I know. I realize how hard this is for you, but there's a reason you can't just let your friendship collapse. Heath cares about you a great deal. He may not realize it now, and he may need to work through this relationship with Diana to figure it out, but the man is not stupid. He will come around, figure out his feelings. And when he does, you have to be there for him. There's no doubt in my mind, or Jace's, that Heath will be lost without you. You don't need to be at his beck-and-call any longer, but don't completely walk away. Meet new people, date, have fun, let Heath see what he's missing."

"You're expecting a lot of both of us. There are no guarantees that Heath's relationship with Diana will fall apart." She paused to take a breath and calm the confusion that had gripped her since his announcement. "He's never once shown any interest in me sexually. I have to accept that there is nothing about me that interests him in that way, as more than a friend."

"You know he may not have thought of you that way because you've never presented yourself as being available, interested in him as more than a friend. Perhaps you've been sending the wrong message."

Annie thought on this a moment even though she believed it wasn't the issue. "You have no idea how much I appreciate your support, but I truly don't believe that's it. The man is focused on women much younger, not on someone two years his senior." She stepped to the window to look out. "The other fact is that no man has approached me in months about dating. I've connected myself so totally to Heath that other men believe we're a couple even though we've both told our friends we're not. And the worst part? The worst part is that the thought of spending time with a man other than Heath holds no appeal for me. None."

Caroline saw the pain in Annie's face. Anger swelled, directed at her brother-in-law. "First, there are no guarantees on anything. I know that as well as anyone." She leaned against the counter and folded her arms across her chest. "There are some people that are so special that it's worth the risk."

Caroline moved back around the kitchen counter into the spacious family room and lowered herself onto the sofa. "You know about the affair Jace had several years ago." Annie nodded. Even though Caroline and Jace had worked it out, stayed together, it was still a painful memory to her friend. "My first reaction was to tell him to leave, go to her if she was who he wanted. I'm glad he walked out before I said a word. It gave us both time to sort out our feelings, decide what we truly wanted."

"I don't know how you did it. If Kit had told me he'd had a one night stand, I don't know what I would've done."

"That was the point. He felt so horrible that he felt compelled to tell me." She leaned forward and placed her arms on her knees. "The truth was, after the miscarriage, I locked him out of my life. I blamed myself, him, anyone else for the fact that I'd lost the baby. Months went by and we hardly spoke, there was no sex. He tried everything, was willing to go through counseling, anything I wanted, but I still refused his love and his friendship."

"You told me he'd gotten drunk at some party and wound up with a young woman you knew. It must have been horrible."

"I refused to go to the party. Shut myself in the guest room, where I'd moved, and told him to go and have as much fun as he wanted. The point is, I was as much to blame as him. He broke promises but so did I by pushing him out of my life. Jace was a mess the next day. I didn't even know he'd stayed out all night until he walked in while I was in the kitchen. He sat down and it just all flowed out. When he was through, he calmly walked into his room, packed some things, and left. Jace didn't call or try to see me for weeks. He came to the ranch, spent time with our boys, worked, met with Heath, but never made any effort to see me. It was brutal, Annie. I finally called him and asked him to stop by. He was living with an older couple in town, hadn't seen the woman again. Jace was as miserable as me, but we realized we were still in love and had to find a way to not only get past his affair but also my blaming him for the miscarriage. It took a long time, but I thank God every day that we worked through it."

This time it was Annie's turn to sit next to Caroline and grab her hand. "Jace is one of the finest men I know and you are his match in every way. I can't imagine either of you with someone else."

"And you are the best thing that's ever happened to Heath, outside of Trey and Cassie. If he doesn't see that yet, give him time, he will. He's a bright guy and he's not about to spend his life with any woman who isn't totally devoted to him. It doesn't take a genius to see how devoted you are to Heath. He just needs time to figure it out."

Annie listened. Caroline had always provided good counsel and sound advice.

If she loved Heath, she should fight for him, as Caroline had done years ago when Jace had strayed. It had broken her heart, almost destroyed their marriage, yet she'd fought for him, and in the end, over the following years, they'd become stronger than ever. Pushing Heath away now would serve no purpose except to drive a wedge between two people who'd already forged a powerful friendship.

"You're right. I do love him, but I won't wait and watch his relationship with Diana grow. I will do my best to still be a friend, but it won't be like before—it can't be."

"That's all anyone can expect. I do think you'll find that in the end, it will be worth it."

"I hope you're right, Caroline. I truly do."

Chapter Nine

"Come in, Annie, and Merry Christmas," Jace leaned over and kissed her cheek then extended his hand to Jake Davison, the man everyone had heard Annie was dating. He was a businessman from Denver who'd met Annie years before when Kit was alive.

"You must be Jake. I'm Jace MacLaren."

Jace took their coats and ushered them into the great room that combined a living room with a family room. It looked into the kitchen and dining room, making for one big entertaining area. The room was filled with people, most that Annie knew. She introduced Jake, grabbed cocktails for each of them, then led him around the giant kitchen island to find Caroline.

They hugged then Annie turned to Jake. "Caroline this is Jake Davison. Jake, I'd like you to meet a close friend, Caroline MacLaren."

"I've heard so much about you, Caroline, that I feel like I know you," Jake commented.

"Same here, Jake. I'm glad you were in town during the party so that I could meet you. Annie told me you don't get to Fire Mountain often."

"No, only since I've become reacquainted with Annie. But I do go to Phoenix every few weeks on business."

"Well, we're only a couple of hours away, so we expect to see more of you."

"Hello, Annie." Everyone turned at the deep voice. Heath stood a few feet away, a beautiful woman holding his arm.

"Hello, Heath. Merry Christmas." Annie turned on her brightest smile, hoping the pain she felt at seeing him for the first time in weeks wasn't apparent. She turned to Jake. "This is Jake Davison."

The men exchanged handshakes.

"Annie and Jake, this is Diana Clements."

"Pleased to meet you, Diana," Jake said.

"Hello, Diana. It's good to meet you." Annie extended her hand. Diana's was cold, like ice even though the room was warm.

Caroline watched Annie struggle. She knew her friend had only spoken with Heath a few times on the phone, and seen him just once, at a board meeting, since he'd told her about Diana. What Caroline also knew was that her brother-in-law was struggling as much as Annie.

"May I get you a refill, Annie?" Jake asked and took the glass from her hand. "Diana, may I get one for you also?"

"I'd love another drink. In fact, I'll come with you," Diana let loose of Heath and linked her arm through Jake's.

"I need to make sure the cook is still setting out fresh food," Caroline said and left the two to themselves.

Heath stared at Annie. She looked incredible. Her blond hair was straight, the way she wore it when it wasn't in a ponytail. She'd done something with her makeup that made her glow and her eyes look huge and round. Her red dress fell off her shoulders and she wore a striking ruby necklace set in gold that rested between her breasts. Heat rose to his face and he felt himself harden. Both feelings, connected with Annie, were a complete surprise.

"You look stunning tonight," he choked out, his voice thick.

"Thank you. You look pretty magnificent yourself." And he did in his black tuxedo with cobalt blue shirt and matching tie.

"I heard you've been dating."

"Yes. Jake called a few weeks ago. He drove from Phoenix a couple of times to have dinner with me. I met him when I was married to Kit."

Heath didn't want details and didn't want to hear anything about a man who was dating Annie. *Is she sleeping with him?*

"Does he stay in Fire Mountain when he comes?" Heath regretted the obvious meaning of his question immediately.

"No. It's not like you and Diana. Not yet at least."

The image of Annie in bed with Jake caused an immediate and sharp pain in the area of Heath's heart. He knew in an instant that the only man who should make love to Annie was him, no one else. *Why haven't I realized this before now?*

"I'd better find Jake, make sure he's comfortable his first time around this crowd."

"Wait, Annie," Heath settled a hand on her arm, stopping her. She looked down then up at him.

"Have coffee with me," he dropped his hand. "We haven't talked in a long time other than the last board meeting and that was all foundation business. There's so much I want to tell you."

She wanted to but couldn't get past the thought that what he wanted was to tell her he'd decided to marry Diana. She just didn't want to hear it while at the same time knowing she had to try to bridge the gap between them. Heath would never be hers in the way she wanted but perhaps they could still have some form of friendship.

"All right but after the holidays. I leave for California in two days to visit the family in San Juan Capistrano and won't be back here until after the first of the year. I'll call you when I get back, I promise."

"All right. Promise accepted."

Annie did call Heath just after the New Year and left a message. He didn't respond.

******

Mid-February

Annie grabbed the phone while sliding into her high heels. She knew it had to be Caroline, confirming once more that she would be attending the charity dance that evening.

"Hi Annie, it's Caroline."

"Hi, Caroline. What's up?"

"Just wanted to know what time you'll be arriving tonight. Are you coming with Jake?"

"No, Jake's in Denver. I'm coming alone. I'll be leaving here in about thirty minutes."

"Good. I'll meet you at the registration table." Caroline sounded breathless, a little edgy, which was uncommon for her.

"No need. I can sign in then find the table."

"I'd rather meet you. We need to talk."

Something was definitely up. "Sure, if that's what you want."

"Call me as soon as you park the car."

"Fine. See you in a bit." Annie hung up and wondered what was going on to cause Caroline to push so hard to meet her in the lobby and not inside. She most likely needed Annie to run interference for someone or agree to be seated at another table. Whatever it was Annie was certain it wasn't as big a deal as Caroline made it out to be.

Thirty-five minutes later Annie pulled into the lot, parked her car, and reached for the cell phone.

"Okay, I'm here."

"Great. I'll meet you in five minutes."

Annie checked in, then waited. Five minutes passed without Caroline walking through the ballroom doors. She waited a few more minutes then decided to forge ahead. Whatever Caroline had to tell her couldn't be that big of a deal. The door to the ballroom flew open and Caroline stepped through.

"Okay, what's going on?" Annie asked.

"Heath's inside. He'll be sitting next to you at dinner."

Annie stared at Caroline, not believing what she'd heard. She had done what she'd promised and called Heath as soon as she'd returned after January first. He hadn't responded. She even tried a second time a couple of weeks later. Still nothing from Heath. It was obvious that he'd decided their friendship wasn't worth continuing.

She'd heard from Caroline that he and Diana had planned to spend a week in the Caribbean in January, then a ski trip to Colorado in early February. It was now late February. It had become clear to Annie that although her friend's advice had been well-intentioned, she'd been wrong. The reality that he truly was lost to her hurt, more so than she cared to accept, even after all these months.

The truth was, she'd never be the type of woman that caught his attention as anyone more than a friend, someone to spend time with when no one else was available. Plus, age was a factor. It was for many men. She'd always be older than him. Annie had accepted that those two qualities were more important than all the friendship, devotion, or love she could provide. He simply did not see her as his type of woman. She'd been relegated to some in-between land, not a woman but not a man. A buddy that fit neither gender.

"I'll find another seat. I'm certain you can locate a single woman who'd be thrilled to sit next to him."

"Annie, he asked to sit next to you."

The request was a surprise but didn't change her mind. "No."

"Please, just listen to me."

"No, Caroline, not this time. I'm not interested in spending a full evening with him. Absolutely not. I'll drive home first."

"He's solo tonight. I think something happened with Diana, but he won't talk to me. Maybe he'll talk to you about it."

"Look, I'm not interested in what happened with Diana, why he's here alone, or why he asked to sit next to me. I just don't care anymore. I'll look for another seat and if none is available, I'll go home. It's that simple." Annie stood her ground. Her words weren't harsh, but this was something which was non-negotiable for her. Heath was out of her life and would stay out. Period.

Caroline stared at her friend. She'd been afraid this was the response she'd get, but hoped otherwise. She walked to the registration table, picked up the seating chart, and studied it, looking for single seats.

"There's nothing. The seat at our table is the last one."

"Don't worry about it, Caroline." She reached over and hugged her friend. "I'll call you tomorrow. Have a wonderful time." Annie slipped back into her coat and turned toward the exit.

"Annie, please, just wait," Caroline called but Annie had already walked through the outside door.

All the way to the car Annie berated herself for being such a coward and felt bad about leaving Caroline to make excuses. Heath had made a decision months ago to pursue a real relationship and he'd chosen Diana. He hadn't known how Annie felt but it wouldn't have mattered if he did. The feelings were one sided, no matter how Annie wished it otherwise.

A foundation board meeting was held in January, but Heath had called in rather than come home from his vacation. The same had happened in February. He was scheduled to be in town for the March meeting. Annie felt certain there'd be no problem continuing her involvement with the foundation. Her feelings would be under control by then.

She drove home, threw her purse on the sofa, and hung up the heavy coat before walking to the sideboard and pulling down the bottle of Maccallan. She poured a small amount into a glass then settled onto the sofa.

Annie hadn't been sure about attending the fundraiser again this year. She'd sent a donation plus the dinner fee, but the whole time juggled the expectation to attend against her desire to avoid the event. Caroline had told her Heath would be attending with Diana, so it wasn't as if it was a surprise. But the tightness in her chest, her inability to take a breath when she heard Heath had come solo did surprise her. Her body's strong reaction took precedence over common sense and she'd run.

When he hadn't returned her calls, Annie had resolved to move on, make other friends, and be open to dating beyond the few dinners she'd shared with Jake. She felt good about where she was and had no intention of backsliding by forcing herself to sit next to Heath, listening to him rave about Diana, and make excuses as to why he'd never returned her calls.

She dated Jake when he was in town and had gone to lunch and dinner with a doctor who'd moved to Fire Mountain over the summer. Annie had met him through Caroline in November.

Barry Newcastle was a good-looking man, divorced, with older children, and a growing practice in orthopedic medicine. She'd had dinner with him a couple of times and was supposed to see him again the following week. Annie liked him, more than she'd anticipated. Barry made her laugh with stories about his training in orthopedics as well as how some people came to be injured. She was looking forward to getting to know him better. Her focus was on the present, not the past, and definitely not on the oldest MacLaren.

Chapter Ten

"Are you going to tell me what's going on?" Jace had come up beside him to stand near a bar at one end of the ballroom.

"One beer and a Jameson on the rocks," Heath told the bartender. He handed the beer to Jace and kept the whiskey for himself. "This isn't a short discussion."

"Caroline's off talking to donors, now is as good a time as any."

The two men walked back to their deserted table. It was close to eleven. Jace, Caroline, and Heath were the only remaining members of their table. Heath looked around the room to see perhaps fifty guests still present, most had left.

"I broke things off with Diana several weeks ago."

The announcement caught Jace by surprise. "You never said anything."

Heath sat back in his chair, holding his glass but not drinking. He looked at his younger brother not knowing how much to say. "It wasn't a hard decision and I felt nothing when I walked away. Not a damn thing." This time he did take a long swallow.

Jace watched confusion then resignation play over Heath's face. It wasn't a secret that he'd never loved his wife, Pamela. He'd told Jace more than once that he'd come to believe that falling in love with a woman was something he had no idea how to do. Jace had found it humorous that a man who could accomplish anything he set his mind to had accepted so easily the concept that love was out of his reach. Even as it was apparent to all how much he loved his children and the other members of the family. The disconnect was obvious to everyone but Heath.

"Yet not being with Annie was a different loss altogether, right?"

Heath's head swung toward Jace and he stared into his brother's eyes. "Yeah, it was."

The two sat in silence as they watched three couples on the dance floor. It was a slow song, the last of the evening. Jace noticed Caroline on the other side of the room speaking with Seth Garner, then moving to another couple. God he loved that woman.

"Does Annie know?"

"That I called it off with Diana?"

"No. That you love her."

It had hit him like a firestorm the night Jace and Caroline had their Christmas party. Heath couldn't take his eyes off Annie, wanted to tell Jake that she belonged to him, not some Denver businessman with no roots in Fire Mountain. He was glad when Diana took Jake's arm and left for another drink. He'd hoped the time alone with Annie would help close the gap that had developed between them, but they'd spoken little, then she'd walked away. The instant feeling of emptiness was like a black hole without a bottom.

He'd forced himself to say nothing to Diana until after the New Year's Eve party her company hosted in Phoenix. After the holidays he couldn't delay the discussion any longer. She took the news well. He'd had the feeling Diana had come to the same conclusion—there'd never be more than what they already had.

Heath had canceled their planned vacations, but instead of letting the family know, he decided to slip off to his cabin in the mountains a couple of hours northeast of Fire Mountain. He focused on work, spent his evenings alone, and plotted on how to get Annie back in his life, permanently.

"I'm not certain I do love her," Heath finally replied.

Jace set his empty beer glass on the table and clasped a hand on Heath's shoulder. "You're so smitten with Annie that you can't think straight. You've been running from it long enough. She's a great woman, perfect for you, and if I'm not mistaken, she's as in love with you as you are with her. Stop wasting time and figure out how you're going to get past the last few months." Jace stood and grabbed Caroline's purse from the table. "I'm going to find my wife and take her home. Then I'm going to spend the next few hours showing her how much she means to me. Just call if you need any advice."

Heath chuckled. "Get the hell out of here and take your gorgeous woman home."

His eyes followed Jace as he made his way to where Caroline stood, saying goodbye to some of the last guests. Jace set his hands on her shoulders, whispered something in her ear then placed a kiss on her neck. Caroline shifted toward him and smiled, then turned to wave at Heath before sliding her arm through her husband's and walking out.

"How could I have missed what everyone else seems to have figured out," Heath muttered to himself.

******

It was late March, five weeks after the fund raiser, and Heath was buried in expansion of the retail property in Phoenix. He'd fielded calls all day from agents interested in representing MacLaren Properties to prospective tenants, investors interested in other projects, and calls from his management team at MacLaren Cattle. Taking a break, he tossed his pen on the desk, sat back, and linked his hands behind his head.

Heath had seen Annie twice, once at the board meeting, where she'd been cordial, and once while he was having lunch downtown with other businessmen. She'd been seated across the room with a man he didn't recognize. He wore dress slacks, a long sleeved shirt, and tie, and appeared to be fascinated by every word Annie said. He kept pushing his blond hair off his face and at one point reached toward Annie to place his hand on top of hers. Heath didn't like the man on sight.

He'd called her twice that week but she never responded. Heath knew that Caroline had told Annie about his split with Diana but it had done nothing to change her mind about renewing their friendship. He hadn't given up but realized rebuilding anything with her would take more time than he'd first thought. He'd been a fool, not recognizing what he had until it was too late.

The phone rang. He would've liked to ignore it but that wasn't an option.

"MacLaren," he said into the receiver.

"Good. You're in the office," Caroline said. "I just spoke with Annie. Something's happened to her son, Eric. He's been in some type of accident. She's determined to drive over there..."

"Where is she now?" Heath was already standing, reaching into his pocket for his keys, and grabbing his jacket."

"Throwing some clothes together, then she plans to leave..."

"I'm on my way now. Call Robert and have him prepare the plane."

"Good. I was hoping you'd say that."

Heath made the drive in record time, jumping from his car, and racing up the front walk. He pounded on the front door. When there was no answer, he grabbed the hidden key, and let himself inside.

"Annie! Are you here?" he called. He looked into the great room, then turned to walk down the hall. "Annie?" he called again.

"In here." Her voice came from the last door down the hall which he guessed was her bedroom. She saw him stop at the entrance, stunned to see him in her house. "How'd you get in?" He held up the spare key. She'd been the one to show him the location last summer. "Look, Heath, I can't talk now. I need to..."

"Pack what you need. We're taking my plane so that you can get to Eric faster."

"But..."

"Don't argue with me on this, Annie. My pilot is already preparing the plane. It will be ready to take off as soon as we board."

She stopped to stare at him. She'd ignored him, refused his attempts to meet, and requests to reconnect. Now he was here, ready to spend who knew how much money getting her to Los Angeles where Eric was undergoing emergency surgery.

"Thank you, Heath," she whispered and closed her suitcase.

He grabbed the bag and headed toward his car.

Robert had the small jet ready, a flight plan filed, and waited their arrival. The plane was in the air twenty minutes after leaving Annie's house.

They sat in silence the first part of the flight, each lost in their own thoughts. Heath knew Annie needed some time to settle down, relax, after the frantic phone call from Eric's roommate.

"Do you feel like telling me what happened?" he asked.

She looked at him, worry and exhaustion apparent on her normally serene face. "I'm not entirely sure. Eric's roommate, Doug, called from the hospital. They'd been riding their motorcycles with a group of friends when a truck came from behind, side-swiped Eric's bike, sending him off the road and down a ravine. He was unconscious when Doug and the others arrived." Her hands shook and she clasped them together in a futile effort to conceal the shaking. He moved next to her and took both hands in his. "They called an ambulance. I don't know what they found, but he's in emergency surgery at the UCLA Medical Center. It was the closest to the accident."

"I know of it. The hospital has a great reputation."

"He celebrated his birthday over the Christmas holiday. I gave him the down payment for the motorcycle. He loved that bike..." her voice trailed off, her hand tightening around Heath's.

Annie looked down at their joined hands, praying that whoever was in charge took good care of her youngest boy. She glanced back up at Heath, tears welling her eyes, pain filled her face. Annie pulled away, resting her hands in her lap and letting her head fall back against the seat. Fear gripped her, the helpless fear of a mother who could do nothing to help her child except pray and make sure the best treatment available was provided.

Heath watched as Annie pulled away and closed her eyes. He couldn't imagine what she was going through. He had yet to experience this type of situation with either Trey or Cassie, and knew Jace had never gone through this with Blake or Brett.

He stood and walked up toward the cockpit, opened the door, and whispered instructions to Robert and his co-pilot. At least he could make sure transportation was available as soon as they landed. The faster they arrived at the hospital the sooner they'd know what was needed to help Eric.

Chapter Eleven

Heath sat, watching Annie pace the small waiting room. He knew how much she hated hospitals, finding it hard to spend time in them.

Eric's roommate, Doug, sat near a window across the room, staring out into the night. Eric was out of surgery and the three were waiting to speak to his doctor. They'd received no answers to their questions on the extent of his injuries or the success of the surgery.

Annie struggled to stay calm knowing that demanding answers wouldn't help. She'd gone through this with Kit during his illness, waiting, praying for a miracle. She hated that she was in the same position again. A hospital was the last place she wanted to be.

Her other children were on their way. Cameron, the oldest, was driving down from his job in Sunnyvale, and Brooke was coming from San Diego where she was finishing grad school. She'd been harder to reach. Annie had finally gotten through to her on the drive to the hospital.

The outside doors burst open, Cameron rushing in and heading straight toward Annie. He grabbed her in a hug then pulled back. "How is he?"

"He's out of surgery but the doctor hasn't come to explain anything."

Cameron nodded then looked past her, noticing Heath for the first time. "Hello, Heath." He walked over and extended his hand.

"It's good to see you, Cameron."

The three looked up when they heard someone approach from further down the hall. He was of average height and wore the standard hospital green clothing. He carried a cup of coffee in one hand.

"Are you Mrs. Sinclair?" he looked toward Annie.

"Yes, I'm Eric's mother."

"I'm Doctor Levine. I performed your son's surgery."

"How is he? Will he be all right?" She worked to keep the panic, and impatience, from her voice.

"Why don't we go in here and talk." He indicated a room to his right. He held the door open while the others walked past and took seats. "Your son had a nasty accident. I don't know the details but the police were here earlier so they'll have more information." He scrubbed a hand over his face then looked at Annie. "Overall, your son is lucky. He has a broken leg, fractured arm, plus numerous cuts and bruises, but there is no sign of internal injuries which is quite rare in this type of accident." He sat back and sipped at his coffee. "We need to keep him in the hospital a few days after he's out of recovery to be sure nothing else is going on."

"No head injury?" Heath asked.

"No. My understanding is that he was wearing one of the full helmets. From the injuries, I'd guess his left side, where the breaks occurred, took most of the impact."

"When can I see him?"

"He should be coming out of the anesthesia within the hour but he'll be groggy. I'll have a nurse let you know as soon as he's awake." The doctor stood. "All and all, your son is a very fortunate young man. None of the injuries are permanent. He'll have some recovery time, but I expect he'll back to normal in a few months." He shook hands and gave Annie an office number if she had more questions.

The four remained in the room after the doctor left. They'd yet to find out any details about the accident. Heath turned to Doug. "Tell us what happened."

Doug was about Eric's age, of medium height, and looked like he hadn't slept in a week. "A group of us were talking. It was a beautiful day and no one had any other classes. Eric was the one to suggest we take a ride—seemed like a great idea." Doug stopped and drew in a shaky breath. Annie knew Doug was a quiet, serious student, finishing his pre-med courses before entering medical school the following year.

"There were eight of us. Everyone is a good rider, no jerks or showoffs. We rode for about an hour then took a two-lane highway toward some restaurant one of the guys knew about. We were heading through an intersection and someone in a truck pulled out from our left, side-swiped a couple of bikes, then raced off. He barely touched one bike, but hit Eric's full-on, sending him off the road. There was about a six-foot drop. Eric landed on his left side and was wedged under the bike. We lifted it off and waited for the ambulance."

"Did anyone get anything on the truck?" Heath asked.

"Two guys rode after him. They got the license plate and make of truck. The police who came to the accident have the information. Don't know how they wouldn't be able to find him." Doug pushed back from his seat and stood. "I need some air."

The others followed Doug out of the small meeting room to find the waiting area full to overflowing. "How about going to the cafeteria?" Heath suggested.

"Sounds good to me," Cameron replied.

"But what if the nurse tries to find us?" Annie didn't want to be too far away from Eric until she'd had a chance to see for herself that he'd be all right.

Heath placed a hand on her shoulder. "I'll let them know where we are and provide my cell number. It's just a floor down according to the map on the wall."

Ten minutes later they were seated in a surprisingly busy cafeteria. Annie and Heath had opted for just coffee while Cameron had grabbed a sandwich and soda. They sat in silence for a while before Annie's cell buzzed. Brooke.

"Hi, Brooke. Where are you?" Annie listened for a few seconds. "We're in the cafeteria on the ground floor." Annie stood to look toward the doors as Brooke entered the cafeteria and waved.

She looks exhausted, Annie thought as she slid her phone back into her pocket.

Brooke dashed over and wrapped her arms around Annie. "How is he?"

"He's going to be all right. We're waiting for the okay to see him."

Cameron hugged his sister then went on to explain what the doctor had told them. "Now we just wait."

Brooke glanced at the table. "I need some coffee." Annie accompanied her to the food line. "What now, Mom? What about school? He's just a few weeks from graduating?"

"I don't have any answers, honey. Right now I'm just grateful he's alive with no permanent damage. We'll work the rest out, we always do." Annie put an arm around her daughter's shoulders then glanced over at their table to see Cameron and Heath talking.

"I was surprised to see you here," Cameron said as he took a bite of his sandwich.

"Why's that?"

"Mom mentioned she hadn't seen much of you the past few months. Told us you'd met someone. That it was pretty serious." He set down his food and crossed his arms.

"It's true that I met someone but that's over—has been for a couple of months."

"I see." Cameron took a big swallow of soda. "We all thought maybe you and Mom had something going. Guess not."

"Would that have been okay with you? If Annie and I had been a couple?"

Cameron considered that a moment. "I never thought about it that way. Mom seemed happy with you, relaxed, like she was before Dad died. You would've had to know her before to see the change. She always made the best of things but nothing could pull her out of the hole she was in after his death. It was tough on all of us, but especially, Mom. Seeing her happy again was all we wanted."

Heath's cell went off as he glanced up to see Annie and Brooke approaching. "Yes?" he said into the phone. "Thanks. We'll be right up." He closed the phone. "Eric's awake."

******

Annie closed the door with a silent click, then leaned her back against it. Eric had been groggy, not able to answer many questions as he continued to nod off every few minutes. They'd stayed just thirty minutes, most of it in silence. It was after midnight and he was sound asleep—at least until another nurse came in to wake him for his next round of medication.

Heath, Cameron, and Brooke stood down the hall, talking, watching her approach. "We'll meet you there," Annie heard Heath tell the others as she walked up to stand next to them.

"We're headed to the hotel, Mom," Brooke said as she gave Annie a brief hug. "We'll meet for breakfast at eight o'clock then come back here, okay?"

Annie looked at Heath.

"We have rooms at the W Hotel just down the street. I've already given the nurse the number there plus she has everyone's cell." He placed a hand on the small of her back to guide her toward the door. "Come on, Annie. You're exhausted."

Heath was right, she was exhausted. A bed and sleep sounded good. Unfortunately, when she closed the door to her room she felt wide awake. She took a few items out of her suitcase, set it on the floor then fell back on the bed. An image of Eric, his left side wrapped in bandages hit her full force. She was so thankful he was alive. Annie didn't think she could lose anyone else.

She rested an arm over her eyes, trying to settle her nerves enough to find sleep. Instead, an image of Heath, holding her hands, putting an arm around her, taking care of everything so effortlessly, came to mind. She'd wanted to wrap her arms around him, pull him close, and never let go. Annie knew that was a fantasy that she alone owned. He didn't feel the same, never would. But he'd been here for them, for Eric, and she'd always be grateful. The phone rang just as she pushed herself up.

"Hello."

"It's Heath. Did I wake you?"

"No. Actually, I'm not that tired. Strange, isn't it?"

"Not really. Coming down from what happened today takes time. Even if your body says it's tired, sometimes your mind doesn't get the message." Heath changed the phone from one ear to the other and propped himself against the headboard.

"Must be the same for you tonight." Annie pulled back the covers, plumped a pillow and sat down.

"That it is."

"I want to thank you again for everything you've done. It's much more than I had any right to expect." Annie felt a lump in her throat, gratitude overwhelming her.

"Why would you not expect my help, Annie?" Heath's voice sounded confused.

"I know you wanted to continue our friendship, have reached out to me lately, and I've avoided you. I'm sorry."

Heath didn't immediately respond. The silence stretched between them.

"How tired are you?" he finally asked.

"Not very, why?"

"I'd like to come to your room, talk for a few minutes if you're up to it." Heath held his breath not at all sure which way she'd answer.

"I guess that would be fine. Would you like some coffee or anything?"

"No, just want to talk. I'll be right there." Heath pulled on a shirt and slipped back into the boots he'd set aside. He grabbed his room key and walked across the hall. He'd made sure Annie was close by.

Annie pulled the door open as soon as she heard the knock. "Hi. Come on in." She stepped aside as Heath walked in and took a seat on the posh sofa.

He leaned back, settling his hands behind his head. His eyes focused on Annie, standing before him, watching uneasily. He let her wrestle with whatever it was that bothered her, not trying to force a conversation. She took a seat in a nearby chair and turned towards him.

"I, um, heard you aren't seeing Diana any longer." She didn't know why that was the first thing to pop out.

"That's right." He continued to watch her, wondering how it had taken him so long to figure out who he wanted was the woman seated before him. For a smart man he'd been a colossal fool. "I knew it wasn't right after a couple of months. Broke it off after New Year's."

"Oh." Annie had so many questions but didn't feel she had the right to ask. "I'm sorry. I know you hoped it would work out for you."

He leaned forward, placing his arms on his knees, and focused on Annie. "I thought Diana was special, but I was wrong. It didn't take long to know she wasn't the woman I wanted."

Annie didn't know how to respond. She felt bad that it didn't work out for Heath and Diana. She'd met her just once, at Caroline's party. Annie had seen why Heath would never be attracted to her the way he was to the picturesque, dark haired beauty.

"Why?" Annie asked.

"Why what?"

"Why did you call it off? She seemed so perfect for you. I know I haven't met most of the women you date, but Diana was a stunning young woman, and from what Caroline said, smart and sophisticated. I would have..." she trailed off, losing her train of thought. She must be more tired than she realized.

"Would have what?"

"I guess you just seemed so right for each other, that's all." Annie stood and grabbed the bottle of water on her nightstand. She took a long swallow.

"We weren't. But there is a woman who is."

Annie stared at him, surprised at how soon he'd found someone else. "Oh, well, I guess that's great. I mean that you've already met someone else. I hope it works out this time." She turned her back to him and paced to the window, opening the curtains to peer out.

"Yeah, I hope so too." He stood and walked the short distance to stand behind her. Annie stiffened when he placed his hands on her waist and pulled her back towards him.

She'd heard him walk up and was surprised to feel his large, strong hands rest on her waist. She knew she should break the contact and put some space between them. When he pulled her back against his chest she was startled at how right it felt, how she wanted to push back further and feel his strength surround her. She began to pull away but he held tight, not letting her move.

Heath knew this wasn't the best time. They were both tired and she was focused on Eric, yet he couldn't stop the overwhelming need to be honest.

He bent his head. "It's you, Annie. I want you," he whispered, his breath sending chills through her. He feathered kisses along the soft column of her neck. When she didn't pull away he let his lips trace a path to her shoulder then back up to the sensitive area behind her ear. She let her head fall back against his chest. He turned her around, moved his hands to cup her face and let his lips caress hers before capturing them in a long, passion filled kiss.

Annie's mind raced. She knew she should push away from him, stop this before she got hurt. But she couldn't. She'd dreamed of this, Heath kissing her, and holding her close, yet never once believed it would happen.

His touch was so much more potent in reality than what she'd imagined. He moved his hands from her face to circle her back, pulling her tight. She moved her hands up his arms, feeling the taught muscles vibrate. She melted into him, her arms wrapping around his neck, pulling him down to her.

Heath wanted much, much more, but not tonight. They were exhausted and Annie was in desperate need of sleep. He'd wanted to take the first step to let her know his feelings towards her, how much he wanted her. If her response to him was any indication, he'd succeeded. He pulled back, resting his forehead against hers and took a ragged breath.

"I don't want to stop, but we both need sleep, and you need to think about what I said, decide if I'm who you want." He released her and stepped back.

Her mind cleared as he spoke. Heath was right. She did need time to rest and time to understand this change in him, his professed desire for her. How had it happened? Was he looking for something permanent or testing the waters?

Annie moved toward the door, gaining more distance, grasped the knob and pulled it open. "Yes, you're right. I'm not thinking so straight, and, well, I don't understand how this change in your feelings happened, or why."

"We'll get Eric taken care of, do whatever is necessary to see that he gets the best treatment and therapy needed—whatever the doctor suggests, then we'll talk about everything. Annie, you need to know I won't change my mind. You've consumed my thoughts for months. You're the reason I let Diana go. I hope in time you'll be able to believe it and perhaps find a way to feel the same for me."

He walked to the door, stopping in front of her. "I'm in love with you, that won't change." He kissed her once more then walked out the door, leaving her to stare after him.

Chapter Twelve

Annie lay in bed. It was five in the morning. She should have been exhausted yet sleep had claimed her for little more than two hours. Her mind kept bouncing between Eric's accident and what would be needed to help him recover, and Heath.

She found it far easier to think about Eric. Her mind couldn't digest what had happened just a few hours before, in this room, with the man she'd wanted for the last year.

Annie looked to the window where she'd been standing when he'd pulled her to him, kissed her, and told her he loved her. It had surprised and scared her, yet not enough to pull away or make him stop.

A few weeks ago, even three days ago she would have pushed him away, demanded an explanation for his sudden change, and been indignant at his pronouncement. Her first reaction would've been to protect herself, her heart. At least she thought those would have been her responses. She certainly hadn't responded that way a few hours ago.

A soft knock had her looking at the clock. Seven in the morning. Where had the last two hours gone?

"Mom, you awake?" Brooke called through the door.

"Yes. Hold on and I'll let you in." Annie climbed out of bed and padded to the door. "Come in and make some coffee. I'll be ready in a few minutes."

"Take your time. We're not meeting Cameron and Heath in the restaurant until eight." She watched her mother stand in place as if waiting for instructions. "Mom, are you all right?"

"What? Um, yes, I'm fine. Just trying to sort some things out." She reached for her clothes on a nearby chair. "I'll take a quick shower and be right out."

Brooke could hear the shower running. It wasn't often that circumstances caused such a change in her mother. Brooke had seen it after her father died. Her mother would move about, stand in one place, then walk a few paces, and sit down. She'd stare in space, not quite seeming to grasp where she belonged or what was expected of her. Her mother was one of the strongest women she knew, a woman Brooke tried to emulate as often as possible. This morning she seemed lost.

The bathroom door opened. "Okay, I think I'm together enough to go downstairs." She threw the last of her things in the suitcase and set it on the floor. "Guess I'll just leave this. I suspect I'll be here another few nights."

The women were escorted to a booth that looked out on a busy street. Annie dug in her purse for her cell phone to check messages. "No message from the hospital. I hope the guys get here soon, I'm anxious to check on Eric." She looked up to see the hostess escort Cameron and Heath to their table.

"Morning, ladies," Heath said, then leaned down to place a kiss on Annie's cheek. "How are you feeling?" He sat next to her, letting his leg touch hers from hip to knee. Her sharp intake of breath wasn't lost on him yet she made no attempt to move away, closer to the window.

"I'm good, Heath. How about you?" Brooke replied when her mother stayed silent.

"Fine. The nurse said Eric had a good night. Doctor Levine was there while I was in the room."

Annie's eyes swung to his at the last comment.

"You were already there? Without me?" Annie's voice was sharp, irritated.

"I walked to the hospital just before five o'clock. You needed your rest and I couldn't sleep." His eyes met hers and held, challenging her to make an issue of his trip down the street. "They let me sit in his room. Eric was awake for a few minutes while the nurse took his vital signs. I don't know how much he'll remember, he was groggy, but I told him we'd all be back between nine and ten." He motioned for the waitress.

They ordered and waited for their food to arrive. Everyone seemed to be showing the effects of little sleep except Heath. He seemed as alert as someone who'd had a full eight hours.

Annie's anger had dissipated somewhat but it was still an irritation that Heath took on a task meant for her. "What did the doctor say?"

"Not much, just that Eric seemed to be doing well. He told me he'd stop back again later this morning." Heath dug into his breakfast then pushed his empty plate away. "I need to make a few calls."

Annie watched him leave, immediately missing the warmth of his leg next to hers. She looked at her own plate and realized she'd just moved the food around and eaten little. "I'm going up to the room then will meet everyone in the lobby in fifteen minutes." She walked toward the elevator then stopped at the sound of Heath's deep voice coming from a narrow hallway. Even though it was wrong, she moved closer.

"No, Diana, I can't make it to Phoenix this week—maybe next. I'm in California." He paused a moment. "It's not your concern what I'm doing here or who's with me. I'll see you when I can." He ended the call, sliding his phone into his jacket pocket. He'd sensed rather than saw Annie behind him and knew she'd heard the conversation.

Annie's heart squeezed at the knowledge he was still making plans to see Diana, even after last night. She dashed around the corner and punched the elevator button, hoping she could make it inside and close the door before he saw her. It wasn't to be.

"I'll ride up with you." Heath stood beside her. The elevator chimed, the door opened, and they both entered, moving to the back wall as the door closed. "In case you're curious, that was Diana." He looked down at Annie. She didn't look up. "She asked me to come to Phoenix to review some modifications to the construction drawings."

Annie bit her lower lip then glanced up at him. "She wants to get back together, doesn't she?"

"Yes."

"Is that what you want?"

Heath turned toward Annie, gripped her shoulders and positioned her in front of him. "Like I said last night, I want you, no one else." He bent and kissed her once, then twice before the elevator chimed once more, signaling they'd reached their floor.

Heath placed a hand on her back and escorted her to the room across from his. "Do you want me to come in?" he asked, a slight smile playing across his face.

"Yes, I mean no." She shook her head and realized he was teasing. "We need to talk about this." Her hand gestured back and forth between the two of them. "Whatever this is."

"Whenever you're ready—just let me know." He left her standing, entered his own room, and shut the door.

******

Three days passed before the doctor released Eric. He was six weeks from graduating, four weeks from finals. His professors had agreed to let Eric complete his final exams online. Heath had arranged for movers. They'd already packed Eric's belongings for the drive to Arizona where he'd stay with his mother until he healed enough to return to California, if that's what he decided.

Eric hadn't applied to grad school as he'd decided months before that he wasn't ready to commit to a specific program. His degree in business would allow him numerous options. He was glad he'd waited. The summer would give him time to determine what he'd do next. He had yet to share with his mother that Heath had already offered him a position with MacLaren Properties.

"Do you need anything, Eric?" Heath asked as his plane made its way home. He sat down near Eric checking to be sure his broken arm and leg were well protected.

"No, I'm fine." Eric glanced to the front of the passenger area of the small private jet. "How's she doing?" He knew his mother worried and hated being the source of what weighed on her now.

"Seems to be doing well now that she knows you'll be okay."

Heath leaned back against the seat and relaxed. Annie had yet to approach him about discussing their future or her desire for one. He had no idea what she was thinking, if his pronouncement had even affected her. He'd learned from Caroline that Annie had been seeing a doctor, someone named Barry Newcastle. According to his sister-in-law, the man was new to town but had already gained the attention of several single women. The doctor's focus was on Annie. Heath meant to change that.

"Doctor Levine said he and Mom had discussed a doctor in Fire Mountain. I don't recall his name." Eric leaned to his right to pick up a glass of water.

"She has a friend who's an orthopedist in Fire Mountain, Dr. Newcastle. Apparently Levine knows him and had already arranged for you to see him." Heath hadn't been thrilled that the doctor was Barry Newcastle. The last thing he wanted was for Annie to spend more time around the man.

The pilot announced they were preparing for landing. Heath checked Eric's setup once again, then settled back for the last few minutes of their flight.

Heath would help Annie get Eric home. After that, he didn't know what to expect. He guessed it was his turn to wait and he'd never been much good at waiting.

Annie sat in front. She'd been watching the late afternoon sky change to deep, vibrant reds and yellows. It was stunning. She glanced to the back where Eric and Heath talked. Annie couldn't hear what they were saying but was thankful they hit it off as well as they did. She owed Heath a lot.

She touched her lips as she'd done numerous times since their brief encounter at the hotel. His interest in her had seemed so sudden, not anything like the platonic friendship they'd shared before. Annie knew he expected to have a conversation with her, explain his feelings, and help her understand the change. She had yet to approach him. Her excuse was Eric and everything that needed to be done. She knew that her son's accident wasn't what stopped her from approaching Heath. It was fear.

Annie knew her feelings for Heath were strong, she was in love with the man. She'd worked hard to accept his relationship with Diana and forge a life without him and their friendship. She'd reconciled herself to his desire for a woman her exact opposite. Now this. What if they tried to make it work but he found he didn't want her as he first thought? What if he realized Diana was the right woman for him after all? Annie didn't know if she could take that chance or the heartache of him walking away.

She did know that Barry was interested. He'd made it clear on their last date that he wanted to take their relationship to the next level. She assumed he meant becoming more serious and sleeping together. That gave her pause. The thought of being with someone other than Heath held no appeal for her.

"Landing in ten minutes, sir," Heath's pilot, Robert, called from the cockpit.

Heath walked to the front and sat down next to Annie, taking her hand, and lacing his fingers through hers. "You're going to have to talk to me about your feelings at some point, Annie. I'm not walking away and I won't stop loving you. You're it for me."

Annie studied their joined hands. "What if I'm not? What if after a while you realize you want Diana back?"

"I won't."

"Then someone else?"

"Not going to happen."

"I'm nothing like the women you've dated. Nothing. I'm older than you, I'm not ..."

Heath didn't let her finish, placing a finger against her lips.

"You're everything I want and need. You. No one else. If you give me time I'll prove it to you."

"Final approach, sir," Robert said.

They didn't speak again until they'd landed and gotten Eric off the plane. Jace and Caroline waited at the airport with their large SUV and helped get Eric settled.

"Guess you'll be staying with Annie," Jace said as he slipped behind the driver's seat.

"That's the plan," Eric responded. His whole body throbbed in pain. He'd declined the last round of pain pills which he now realized was probably a mistake.

Heath stood nearby. His car was still at the airport, the one he'd used to pick up Annie several days ago for the trip to the airport. He knew he'd be leaving the airport alone as he watched Annie climb into the SUV next to Eric. She nodded to Heath as she shut the door. She hadn't said goodbye.

Heath watched Jace pull away and the most profound feeling of loss he'd ever experienced overtook him. He realized that for the first time in his life he'd found love and had no control over whether or not the woman he wanted would accept him. He felt vulnerable, exposed—a feeling he didn't like one bit.

Chapter Thirteen

A week had passed without any word from Annie. No calls, emails, texts—nothing. Heath focused on work and the need to keep his numerous projects moving forward while his personal life stayed on hold. A week wasn't much, he kept telling himself, yet it felt like a lifetime now that he'd finally told Annie of his feelings.

"You ready?" Jace asked as he poked his head into Heath's office.

"Ready for what?"

Jace would've laughed if he didn't know his brother was struggling with his feelings for Annie. He knew Heath had told her how he felt and knew that Annie hadn't responded. Life could be a bitch.

"The foundation board meeting, in the conference room, now."

Heath had forgotten. He stood, grabbed the meeting folder, and started out the door, realizing that Annie would be at the meeting. His anticipation grew.

They walked into the conference room which Heath quickly scanned. No Annie.

"Are we waiting for Annie?" he asked Caroline who was the only person Annie had connected with the last week.

Caroline kept her eyes down, pretending to study the documents in front of her. "No. She called to say she won't be able to make it. The orthopedist wants to see Eric again today and this was the only time available."

The orthopedist. Barry Newcastle. Heath took the news with no noticeable reaction and sat down.

"Let's get started."

Two hours later he sat once more in his office except this time he held a glass of Jameson in his hand while across the desk from him Jace held his own.

"What are you going to do?" his brother asked.

"I don't know." Heath didn't pretend Jace's meaning wasn't clear. "At least she stays in touch with Caroline. That's something." He tossed down the amber liquid and poured another two fingers.

"Well, she's not seeing the businessman from Denver any longer. That was over a couple of months ago. The only other person Caroline's mentioned is the doctor. According to my wife, that one's not serious."

Heath wasn't so sure of that. He'd been having dinner with a couple of friends two nights before and seen Annie, and the good doctor, walk into the Italian restaurant next door. He'd felt as if a baseball bat had connected with his chest. Full force, no holding back.

"Perhaps not, but I'm not chancing it."

"What do you intend to do?"

"What I should have done a year ago. Ask her out?"

"You're going to start dating her?" Jace was surprised. He didn't think it was a tactic Heath would use.

"Why not? It's what you did when you were trying to win Caroline back. As I recall, it worked."

"That it did," Jace smiled. "Best thing I ever did was woo her like I did in high school. She couldn't resist me either time." He knew there was a lot more to their reuniting the second time yet chose to focus on the good parts of their reconciliation

"I hope it works as well for me."

Jace held up his glass and tilted it toward Heath. "I wish you luck."

"Thanks. I'm going to need it."

******

"Mom, aren't you going to return Heath's calls. It's the third message he's left at the house and I'm guessing he's probably done the same on your cell." Eric had heard each message as it came into the answering machine at home.

She needed more time to figure out her feelings, particularly the fear that gripped her, and decide if she could take a chance on the all too eligible Heath MacLaren. He was everything she wanted yet she couldn't shake the voices in her head telling her to be cautious.

"Of course I'll call him back. I've just been busy between your doctor appointments, my writing schedule, and the other things I have going."

"Like dinner with Dr. Newcastle?" It wasn't said in a judgmental way, yet Annie thought she'd heard a certain amount of censure in her son's voice.

"He's a nice man and we had plans even before your accident. The man is new in town, looking to meet more people, and..."

"Safe?" Eric asked.

"Well, yes."

"Not like Heath who has the horrible burden of sorting through too many gorgeous women who'd like nothing better than to marry the wealthy rancher."

"I guess."

"Mom, it's time you face something here. The man is crazy about you. Even I could see it at the hospital and I was loopy on drugs half the time. He couldn't care less about anyone else, just you." He was quiet for a minute. Cameron, Brooke, and he just wanted her to be happy, like she was when their father was alive. Her friendship with Heath made her happy, at least until he'd taken that detour for a few months. "Give the guy a chance. I think he'll surprise you."

"I don't know, Eric. It seemed so much easier when he just wanted to be friends. Anyway, I've already committed to going to dinner with Barry tomorrow night plus a fundraiser next weekend. It wouldn't be right to cancel now."

"Whatever you think, Mom. God knows I'm lousy at this type of stuff." Eric adjusted the reclining chair a little and picked up the television remote, flipping through stations until he settled on the Military Channel.

Annie knew what her son meant. He'd had one serious relationship, his high school sweetheart. They'd gone off to USC at the same time and had been an item, planned on getting married, up until a year ago when she announced she'd started seeing a grad student in the engineering department. It had been a devastating blow to Eric.

Eric looked at Annie the minute the house phone started to ring. "Well?"

She made a slight face and grabbed the receiver. "Hello."

"So you are still around." Heath.

"Hello, Heath," she glanced again at Eric who sported a self-satisfied grin.

""What are you doing tonight?"

"Nothing other than warming up dinner for Eric and me."

Eric motioned to her with his hands, telling her to take off, do whatever Heath suggested.

"If it's not too late, I'd like to invite you to dinner. If you feel like it, we'll go to that place you like with the peach cobbler afterwards." For the first time Annie heard the nervous tone in Heath's voice.

"Are you asking me out, like a date?" She couldn't hide the hope that her guess was right.

"Yes, I am. I know it's old fashioned but I want to court you, Annie. Maybe then you'll believe how serious I am."

She stood silent, still not quite believing that Heath was truly serious about her.

"I'd like that," was all she could get out.

"Great. How is seven o'clock?"

"Good. Perfect."

"I'll see you then," he paused a moment. "And, Annie, thanks." He clicked off.

Her heart was beating so fast and hard she thought it would disintegrate from too much effort.

"I take it I'm on my own tonight?" Eric's eyes never left the television screen.

"Guess so. Hope that's all right."

His head swung toward her. "Are you kidding? A night alone without parental guidance. What more could any college senior ask for?" A smile filled his face.

Annie warmed up the dinner she'd already prepared and handed Eric a plate before dashing down the hall to clean up. She had a new pair of sleek, tight-fitting, black silk pants, a beautiful peach colored blouse with a low v-neck, and three inch heels. She hoped he was ready for her.

******

Heath knocked at exactly seven o'clock.

"Come on in, Heath," Eric shouted and watched as the door swung open. His mother's date walked in and placed his hat on a hook in the entry.

"You look a damn sight better than you did a week ago. How are you feeling?" Heath held out his hand, which Eric accepted.

"Pretty good, given the circumstances." He nodded toward the hall. "I haven't seen her since she hung up the phone with you. Grab yourself a drink and have a seat. Who knows how long it will be. Unless you've already exceeded your quota of liquid courage."

Heath chuckled at the accuracy of Eric's statement. He had reached his limit. It had taken two whiskeys and a shove from Jace to get him to pick up the phone.

The men looked up as Annie approached. She stopped just inside the family room, unaware that Heath had already arrived.

"Oh, hello, Heath."

Heath didn't answer. He was still trying to close his jaw which had dropped to the floor at the sight of her. *Shit*, he thought and his mouth went dry. She was stunning.

"Heath, are you all right?" The distress in Annie's voice was real. Maybe she didn't look as good as she thought.

"Yes, I'm fine," Heath's voice was low, thick. "You look gorgeous, Annie." He walked over and placed a kiss on her cheek.

"I hope it's all right for what you planned."

"Oh, it's better than all right. Way better." He turned to Eric. "Guess we'd better get going. Anything you need before I steal your mother away?"

"Nope, I'm good. Got my chair right here, the channel changer, a soda, and bag of chips. Life's good."

Annie placed a kiss on Eric's cheek. "Call if you need anything."

"Don't worry about me. You two have fun and behave yourselves. Curfew is ten, well maybe eleven."

Smart ass, Heath mouthed as he led Annie to the door and outside before helping her into his car.

Heath walked around and climbed into the driver's seat before turning to Annie. "You look truly gorgeous tonight, you know that?" He leaned over, placed a hand behind her head, and brushed her lips with his. He pulled back a fraction, then took her mouth again, this time with more urgency, sweeping inside to taste her. He pulled back. "I've waited all week for that." His eyes darkened and his voice had grown rough.

Annie cleared her throat and she straightened in her seat. "So, where are we going?"

He started the car, backed out, and turned toward town. "Sheldon's, if that's all right."

She loved Sheldon's and he knew it. "It's better than all right." She turned a bright smile toward him.

Her smile was like a bolt of lightning to his system. "Music?" he asked before he said something stupid, like, *dump the doctor, you're mine.* He needed to settle down, get a grip.

He used the valet parking and escorted Annie inside. Their table was ready, a quiet corner in the back that Heath had requested. They passed several people they knew and said their hellos before Heath's warm hand on her back pressed her towards their table. He didn't want to waste a moment of this night with anyone except Annie.

They perused the menu, which was just a formality as the few times they'd come here each had ordered the same thing.

"What may I get you tonight?" the waiter asked.

"Lamb," both answered in unison, looked at each other, and laughed.

"Good choice," the waiter grinned, took the rest of their order then left them alone.

Heath held up his glass of wine toward Annie. "To many more nights like this."

Annie touched his glass and hoped it was so.

Chapter Fourteen

"Okay, give. How was your date?" Caroline asked as she sat outside on Annie's deck juggling a glass of ice tea in one hand and a list of things she needed to go over with her friend in the other.

Annie thought of last night and a warm feeling passed through her. "It was wonderful."

"And has he told you he loves you?"

"He told me that over a week ago in Los Angeles."

"What? And I'm learning about this now?" Caroline looked a little put out yet Annie knew it was partly an act.

"I wasn't sure he meant it knowing how he felt about relationships." She ran a hand through her long, blond hair and thought about going inside to put it up in a ponytail until her cell phone rang. She dug it out of her pocket and answered. "Hello."

"Hi."

It's Heath, she mouthed to Caroline. "Hi, yourself. What's going on?"

"Nothing, at least not at the moment. There was a lot to take care of this morning, now it's quiet." He paused. "Guess I just wanted to hear your voice."

Her gut clenched at the knowledge that he'd missed her, wanted to talk. "I had a wonderful time last night."

"Then how about tonight?"

Annie hesitated as she realized she had a date with Barry tonight. "I'd love to but I have other plans."

The silence stretched on. Annie worried her lower lip. It was too late to cancel yet she wanted to be with Heath, not on some date with a man she liked but didn't love.

"Heath, are you still there?"

"Yeah. Another date with the doctor?" His voice had grown hard and she could feel the tension build even over the cell lines.

"Yes, with Barry."

"I guess I'd better let you go. I'm sure you have lots to do before tonight."

"Not that much. It's casual, dinner at Jersey's. Nothing special." She hoped he could hear the regret in her voice.

"Another time."

"Yes, another time."

"I'd better get going. Talk with you later." He hung up.

Heath stared at the phone before pushing his chair back to stand. They'd had a good, no, a great time last night. He'd pulled off the road a block before her house and they'd necked like teenagers. It had taken every ounce of will power he possessed to not take her right there, in the front seat of his car. She'd been sweet, clung to him when he kissed her goodnight, then waved when she closed the front door. Now this.

His disappointment was acute. Heath was more than ready to move forward with this, have as many dates as needed to get her to believe his feelings for her were real. He could direct companies, make each business a virtual money machine, lead hundreds of employees, yet he couldn't find a way to get one woman to believe he loved her. Worse yet, he couldn't figure out why she was still dating the local doctor. He'd wait a few days and try again, give her time to think about what she wanted.

Annie heard the click and looked down at her cell to see the call had ended. All the joy she'd felt from last night fled as quickly as the end of his call. She sat back and stared out at the grove of trees in her back yard. Sitting on the deck always relaxed her, today it made her edgy. Annie didn't understand why she hadn't said yes and called Barry to cancel the date. It would never go anywhere, not with her feelings for Heath.

She and Barry had kissed twice. Each one brief yet she'd felt none of the passion or desire to pull him close like she did with Heath. If they ever did make love she was afraid she'd devour Heath. She smiled at the thought.

"I'm guessing he wasn't happy about you seeing the doctor tonight."

"No, not happy at all." She looked at Caroline. "What am I to do? I'd feel horrible canceling dinner tonight, yet I don't want to go. If Heath does love me I don't want to spend another moment with someone else."

Caroline set down her tea. "You're right, you can't cancel, but you can use it as an opportunity."

"Opportunity?"

"To tell the doctor you're in love with someone else."

She'd have to tell Barry sometime, and she'd never do it over the phone, so why not tonight?

"Of course." She hugged her friend. "That's a brilliant idea."

"Good. Now that that's settled, I have a list of stuff to go over with you."

******

"You look lovely tonight, Annie," Barry said when she met him in front of the restaurant. He'd been held up at the hospital and called to ask if she'd be okay meeting him. That was perfect. She wasn't looking forward to him taking her home after learning they'd just had their last night out.

"Thank you. I know Jersey's is casual."

They walked inside and took a table by the front window where they could watch the goings on across the street in the town square.

"Long day?" Annie asked.

"Yes, very. A member of the high school baseball team slid into home and broke his leg in two places. Nasty business. I hate this part of my job, watching young people get injured in a way that will impact the rest of their lives. His playing days may be over." He sipped his wine and continued to stare out the window.

"The good news is that you're good at what you do. If any doctor can give the kid another chance, you can. He got the best treatment available, doctor." Annie held up her glass and toasted him.

He offered a tired smile. "Perhaps this wasn't such a good idea. I may not be the best company."

Annie thought of waiting, but now seemed like the opening she needed. They hadn't ordered dinner, he was tired, wanting to get home, and she needed to unburden her heart.

"Barry, I need to say something."

He turned his gaze from the window and focused on her. "This doesn't sound good."

They weren't in love but she was fond of him, didn't want to cause him hurt.

"Do you remember when I told you I had a friendship with Heath MacLaren?"

"The rancher who flew you to Los Angeles?"

"Yes, that's him. Well, as it turns out, we've just realized we're in love."

Barry watched her a moment then let out a deep sigh. "I didn't realize you'd seen much of him lately."

"I haven't and that's probably why this came about. Both of us needed space to realize our friendship was so much deeper than we'd thought. Strong enough that neither has a desire to be with someone else. I'm sorry, Barry. I hope you understand."

He reached over and placed his hand on hers. "Annie, as long as you're sure, then yes, I understand."

She started to rise but he held tight to her hand.

"You'll call me if you change your mind?"

"Yes, I'll call." He was a good man, kind and compassionate. Being with him was an honor.

He stood and placed a kiss on her cheek. "Best to you, Annie, and to Heath. I know you'll make it work."

"Thanks, Barry." She started toward the door. "You know you'll still be seeing me when I bring Eric in for his exams."

"I'll look forward to it. Goodnight, Annie." He sat down and turned back to the window.

******

Annie drove home, restless yet glad she'd ended it with Barry. Now she could concentrate on Heath. Her heart jolted at the thought that they might truly work this out and create a life together.

She walked in the front door and saw that Eric had already hauled himself down the hall to his bedroom. He hated feeling helpless. The first thing he did after the doctor gave his approval was to practice getting in and out of his wheelchair with most of his left side in casts. He'd learned how to position the chair, leveraging with his good right side, and sliding into the seat in one smooth movement. Annie was stunned the first time he'd showed her.

She poked her head into his room. He was already asleep even though it was still early. Annie knew he'd started studying for finals, which were just a couple of weeks away. At least he could take them online.

Annie turned off the lights before making her way to her own room. She undressed and crawled under the covers, grabbing a book and settling against the headboard.

It was hard to concentrate on the story even though it was good. Her mind kept wandering to Heath and what his response would be when she told him about her conversation with the doctor. She couldn't believe how excited she was to speak with him tomorrow. Annie knew he'd call and looked forward to whatever he had planned.

Heath didn't call the next day or the following. No texts, no emails. She'd decided he needed to make the next move even as her mind told her to call him, explain what had happened.

Friday night came and went, and still no word from him.

"He'll call, Mom. He's just a busy guy," Eric had assured her.

Saturday morning dawned with clear skies and brilliant sun. Annie woke at six and dressed for a workout before settling into her office to work. She had no plans, having kept herself open for whatever Heath had planned.

By five o'clock that afternoon and no word from him, she decided to gather her courage and drive to his place. She wouldn't call, just show up to talk. It would be fine, she was sure of it.

*****

Annie showered, dressed, forced down some fruit then grabbed her keys. It was almost eight o'clock. She'd decided to give him more time to call. He hadn't.

It was a twenty minute drive to his front door. She saw a new sports car out front but didn't think anything of it and parked her small SUV. She reached for her purse, checked her image in the mirror, and satisfied, walked to the front porch. It took her a couple of deeps breaths before she wound up the courage to knock.

It took a minute before the door was yanked open. "Yeah?" It was Heath. He wore trousers but no shirt and his feet were bare. He held the door open but had yet to look at who'd knocked. Finally he turned to see Annie. "Annie? What are you doing here?"

"I thought we could talk, that is if you have some time." Something wasn't right, she could feel it.

"Now may not be the best time..." Heath started before a voice from inside interrupted him.

"Heath?"

Annie looked behind Heath to see Diana in an almost there outfit, barefoot, and holding a bottle of wine in one hand.

Reality dawned like a sledgehammer to her solar plexus. The intense pain almost doubled her over. She stepped back from the door.

"I, uh, I guess this is a bad..." she couldn't even get it out before she turned and ran. Tears already filled her eyes, blurring her vision.

"Annie wait! Don't leave, please!"

She could barely hear his voice. The ringing in her ears made it sound as if she were in a tunnel. Her head began to spin as she opened the car door to climb behind the wheel. She fumbled with her keys. She looked up to see Heath dashing outside. He'd grabbed a shirt and was buttoning it as he made his way to her car.

"Annie! Don't go. Let me explain."

Explain? Her mind screamed. She couldn't draw a breath, couldn't think. She had to get out of there. Annie tried once more to put the key in the ignition. It slid in. She turned the key, put the car in gear, and pushed hard on the accelerator, fishing tailing and barely missing Heath as he ran around to cut her off.

She gunned the engine and blew past him as tears streaked down her face. She didn't look back and didn't stop even as she could still hear his shouts behind her. What a fool she'd been, believing he loved her.

Annie drove a few miles then pulled over. She couldn't see for the tears that blurred everything in sight. She turned off the engine and lights then sat back in the seat until her head and eyes had cleared. Every part of her ached as if she'd been slammed by a moving train. Minutes passed. She started the car and made her way home, continuing to berate herself for believing in someone incapable of love or the commitment that went with it.

Annie pulled into the garage and walked inside, throwing her purse on the counter before grabbing a glass of water. She chugged it down and took several deep breaths. That's when she heard it. The sound of a truck stopping in her drive.

She dashed to the window to see Heath getting out and heading straight for her door. He didn't knock, just grabbed the spare key, and walked inside.

Annie stood not ten feet away, her red face and puffy eyes all the confirmation he needed that he'd made a huge mistake opening the door to Diana that night.

It had been close to seven o'clock. Heath had showered, pulled on a pair of jeans, and settled into a comfortable chair in the family room. He'd been ready to call Annie, find out what was going on, and get her to commit to seeing him tomorrow, maybe tonight if he could talk her into it. Pounding on the front door had stopped him.

He'd opened the door to find Diana in one of her sleek, suggestive outfits standing outside with a bottle of wine in one hand and take-out in the other.

"What are you doing here?" he'd asked, none too gently.

"Why? Aren't you glad to see me?"

"No, not at all. What do you want?" He'd held the door firm, not letting her pass.

"Why, I drove all this way just to see you. You're alone, I'm alone. I thought we might be able to find something to fill our time."

"No, Diana, it's over—we're over." Frustration gripped him. "There's someone else and she's important to me. They'll be no more you and I, understand?" He'd been furious at Diana. She just wouldn't let go even though she'd shown no signs of being upset when he'd called it off months before. The last few weeks he'd had to field numerous calls from her. Now this.

She'd stood in silence for a moment, digesting his words, then raised her head, her trademark smile plastered on her face. "Oh, all right. But at least let me come in and use your bathroom before forcing me back out on the road."

He still didn't want to let her in, something told him not to, yet the gentleman in him won over the certainty that it was a mistake.

Diana had no more come out of the bathroom and begun to gather her things when someone else knocked at his door. He'd pulled it open to see Annie. *God, could this get any worse?*

Now he stood in Annie's house. The two of them staring at each other.

Heath broke the silence. "You are going to let me explain."

"There's nothing to explain. I'm pretty sure I understand what was going on."

"No, you don't understand. That's why you're going to let me tell you."

"No."

He walked towards her and gripped her shoulders, forcing her to meet his gaze. "Annie, I love you. No one else. You're going to let me explain what was going on at my place, then we're going to talk it through. After that, you're going to tell me why in the hell you haven't called it off with the doctor."

She couldn't remember ever seeing Heath this angry. Maybe something else had been going on. Annie calmed enough to realize he was right. She didn't know what had happened, only drawn conclusions from the very graphic image Diana presented. She owed him the chance to explain.

"All right. You can explain. After that you'll have to leave."

He would settle for that—for now.

She walked to the kitchen and started some tea. "Coffee, anything?"

"Coffee would be great. Thanks." Heath took a seat on the other side of the counter. "Where's Eric?" He'd expected to see the young man in his normal spot on the sofa.

"Doug and a couple of friends from school drove over for a few days. They got rooms at a hotel. Told Eric he needed some time away from home and hauled him off. Kind of quiet without him."

Annie handed Heath his coffee, grabbed her cup, and sat on a nearby stool.

"Okay. Explain."

It didn't take more than fifteen minutes for him to describe the break-up, Diana's repeated attempts to reconnect, her uninvited appearance at his home that night, and how he'd had to wait for Diana to drive away before he could follow Annie. He paused to push both hands through his thick, dark hair then stood and walked to the large, plate-glass window. It was a dark night with the sliver of a moon peeking through the tall pines in Annie's backyard. He turned from the window and shoved both hands in the pockets of his jeans, his expression bleak.

Annie felt horrible about judging him before getting the facts. Yet, it had seemed so clear when she'd looked behind him to see Diana with a smirk on her face. Now it all made sense.

"I guess I may have overreacted."

"You guess?"

"All right, I did overreact, but I think you might have done the same in my position."

"Perhaps." Heath's heated gaze locked on her. "Now, the doctor. I want to know why you're still seeing him." He'd stepped within two feet of her.

She jumped from the stool and walked around the counter into the kitchen. "The doctor. Well, he's a good man, dependable, kind." She looked up at Heath. "You know, all the things a woman wants."

Heath followed her at a slow pace, not letting her get more than a few feet away. "Everything a woman wants?"

She took a deep breath. "Of course, not every man can offer all a woman wants." Annie moved to the sink, then around the center island to the counter on the other side.

"Are you sleeping with him?"

"No, of course not."

Relief washed over him. "Do you feel the same way with him as you do with me when we kiss?" He continued following her around the kitchen, crowding her space.

"Well, not really. It doesn't matter anyway." The room felt hot. She'd have to check to see if Eric had changed the setting.

"Why's that?"

"I called it off with him tonight. That's why I drove out to see you, to let you know." Annie moved into the family room, trying to create some distance.

"So, it's just you and me now, Annie. No doctor and no one else, right?"

"No, no one else." She'd backed up against a wall. Heath now stood not a foot away. "I don't understand what you want from me," she whispered.

He took another step forward, placing his hands against the wall on either side of her. "Oh, I think you do." He dipped his head and captured her mouth in a searing kiss, increasing the pressure when he heard her soft moan.

Heath wrapped his arms around her, tangling his hands in her hair, and shifting his mouth one way then another before delving inside to taste her. A hand trailed down her back to her hip, resting a moment before moving upward, caressing her through the thin blouse. He flipped open the buttons then pushed her top aside before reaching behind her to unhook her bra. He let both fall to the floor as his mouth returned to her neck and sought the soft spot under her ear.

Annie could barely breathe, the sensations at his touch creating a heat that grew with each caress. She pulled his head down and held him to her, wanting to wrap herself around him, mold their bodies together and become a part of him.

"Annie, I want you tonight, now."

"Yes."

He didn't wait but lifted her into his arms, not breaking contact with her mouth, and carried her down the hall to her bedroom.

******

They'd made love for what seemed like hours, touching and holding each other after each was totally spent. Heath had never felt this way—complete—as if Annie was a part of his being that couldn't be separated without causing irreparable damage.

Heath pulled her tight against his chest not wanting to sever the contact. He nuzzled his face in her hair and trailed kisses down her neck to her shoulders.

"I want a second chance with you, a second summer, and every summer after that," he whispered.

Her eyes slowly opened as his words washed over her. "What are you asking?" she breathed out.

"I'm offering you all I have, Annie. Marry me."

Annie turned to face him and wrapped her arms around his neck.

"You're certain? You won't change your mind?"

"Never. I'm yours."

Chapter Fifteen

Two months later...

The wedding came together easily. Annie and Heath wanted the same thing—close family and friends at a beautiful site on the ranch that overlooked the valley and the magnificent mountains beyond.

Everyone was to meet in a few hours using horses, wagon, or walking. No cars allowed. The MacLarens supplied the transportation for those who wanted to ride or guests to use their own. Tents had been erected, just in case the weather turned nasty. After the ceremony, everyone would ride back to the ranch for a light supper that Caroline had arranged. It was, for Annie and Heath, the perfect wedding.

"I can't believe Annie bought into Caroline's argument," Heath complained as Jace helped him with the last of the provisions needed on their ride. He hadn't seen or slept with Annie in six days, almost a week, and it showed. After not sleeping apart for almost two months the separation was a true irritant.

"Look at the bright side," Jace chided. "Think how great it will be tonight after a week of drought." He chuckled and started toward the house.

Heath watched Jace walk away, hating the separation. They were adults, for crying out loud, on their second marriages. They'd been sleeping together for weeks. Why in hell would Annie agree with Caroline that a few days apart would give them a fresh start? Annie was his fresh start. He didn't need any separation to figure that out.

Jace trudged out carrying one last satchel filled with items Caroline had said they'd need at the ceremony. He placed it in the wagon. One of their men would drive it out to the site once Eric arrived.

"Look there," Jace nodded toward the long driveway.

"Must be Eric and his friends." Heath waved then waited for the truck to park in front of the house.

Doug jumped out, offering his hand to Heath and Jace.

"How you doing, Doug? I see you brought your other miscreant friends with you," Heath chuckled as he walked up to the truck and opened the door to help Eric out. The cast had come off his arm a couple of weeks before but he still had to wrestle with the cast on his leg. Three to five more weeks Barry Newcastle had told him.

Heath had helped Annie take Eric to the doctor's office for one of his exams. He and Barry had spoken briefly, the doctor offering his congratulations on the upcoming wedding but warning Heath that if it didn't work out, Barry would be waiting. At least the doctor was honest.

"You going to be all right riding in the wagon?" Heath asked Eric. "If not, we can get a car out there."

"Are you kidding, and risk the wrath of my mother? No, she said no cars and I'm not going to be the one who goes against her."

"Smart choice." Heath and Jace helped him up on the wagon seat while Doug and their other friends climbed into the open spaces behind.

"All right, you're off." Heath stood by to watch the wagon move north toward the wedding site. He estimated it would take them no more than thirty minutes by wagon. "When do the ladies get here?" he asked Jace who was just hanging up his cell phone after a call with his oldest, Blake.

"Didn't Annie tell you that they'll meet us out there?"

Heath stared at his brother, placed his hands on his hips then turned toward the house.

"Hey, it's not my fault you didn't get the memo," Jace called after him and chuckled. He'd never seen Heath in such unfamiliar territory. Control had been stripped from him as well as his woman. *Life just keeps getting better* Jace grinned as he headed to the barn and the horses.

******

An hour later everyone was gathered on the vista overlooking the valley. There was a lake in the distance and much of the surrounding pastureland was green from the heavy spring rains. Heath looked around. Annie wasn't anywhere in sight.

"She'll be here." Jace clapped a hand on his brother's shoulder.

"Yeah, I know." Heath tried to stay positive yet a niggling sensation warned him that perhaps she'd changed her mind and decided marrying someone who had a history such as his wasn't worth the risk.

"She's crazy about you," Jace continued, looking around and wondering what was taking the women so long.

"Yeah, I know." He'd never been insecure, hardly knew what the word meant, yet he felt apprehensive and anxious. This was either going to be the best or worst day of his life. All he could do was wait to see which.

"They're coming!" Jace's youngest son, Brett, called out from his perch on a nearby hill.

Heath closed his eyes and let out a deep breath—glad none of his business associates had been invited. He sure as hell didn't want them to see him like this.

A few minutes later a beautiful black carriage rolled toward him, his son Trey driving with Cameron sitting alongside. He brought it to a perfect stop just feet away from where Heath stood.

Jace opened the carriage door, helping Brooke, Cassie, and finally Caroline, the matron of honor, descend. He motioned for Heath.

He took one hesitant step, glanced at Trey who nodded to him to get moving, then closed the distance to the carriage and looked inside.

A beautiful sight, a vision really, smiled back at him. He held out his hand. When she accepted it a wave of feelings passed through him like nothing he'd ever felt. He saw his future in that brief moment and an understanding that everything he'd ever dreamed of was now his.

Annie stepped down, holding tight to Heath's hand. Music began to play and the couple turned toward their guests.

"Wow." Blake turned to his younger brother, Brett. "She looks great."

The music continued as Jace and Caroline walked, arm and arm, to where the minister stood, his back to a majestic combination of meadows, water, and mountains. They stopped and turned toward the bride and groom.

Heath smiled at Annie as he led her forward, trying to concentrate and not be distracted by the beautiful woman on his arm.

The minister watched them walk forward. He'd seen many brides yet Annie stood out in a class by herself. She wore a beautiful cream colored lace and silk gown that fell off her shoulders. Lace sleeves continued down her arms, ending in a vee at her wrist. The skirt fell in soft vees to just below the tops of the Victorian western lace-up boots she wore. Her ivory colored silk western hat was adorned with lace and pearls, with a veil that fell to her mid-back.

The music stopped. Annie and Heath dropped their hands to take a small step apart, each smiled, then looked up at the minister.

"Dearly beloved..."

Epilogue

"I'm so glad you were able to make it out, Trey. I know Heath hoped you could get the time even if he never said it." Annie followed her new stepson outside. He was flying back to NAS Lemoore.

"There wasn't a problem getting away. I wouldn't have missed it." He leaned down to give Annie a kiss on the cheek before sliding in next to Heath for the drive to the small air field near Fire Mountain. Robert would fly him to California. He'd be back on base in a couple of hours.

"See you in a bit," Heath said to Annie as he pulled away.

Annie watched them leave then turned to walk into the big ranch house that had become her home. She made tea and settled in a large, leather chair that had been in the family for two generations and reflected on the last few weeks.

She was now the mother of three and step-mother of two. She loved them all which meant now there were two more to worry about. Annie laughed at her train of thought. There were also two more she'd be allowed to watch build their lives as well as their own families. She set the cup down, wrapped her arms around a pillow, and nodded off.

Heath stood by the plane, giving the final instructions to Robert while Trey threw in his one bag. He was proud of his son, of what he'd achieved, yet each goodbye seemed more difficult. Something was weighing on Trey. He'd refused to confide in either his sister, Jace, or him. That was the hardest part. Knowing Trey carried a burden he was unable or unwilling to share.

"Thanks, Dad," Trey wrapped his arms around his father and pulled tight. None of this attaboy type stuff for them.

"You be safe and let me know how things are going," Heath replied and stepped back. "Annie and I will look forward to all the calls and letters." Both grinned, knowing that Trey was bad at both.

"Text all right?"

"Sure, we'll accept texts."

Trey started up the steps then turned back. "Annie is a great woman. You're lucky to have her."

"Yeah, I know." Heath stepped back as the door closed, locking Trey inside. It would be months before they saw each other again.

He walked to his car and stood until the plane taxied out then took off, waving, knowing Trey was waving back. Heath bent down to get into the car, put the key in the ignition, and smiled. Time to grab his bride and start getting ready for their two-week honeymoon in Paris.

Trey watched as the plane lifted off, leaving his father waving from the ground. He loved his dad, wished he could've told him what was happening, knowing it wasn't an option since he wasn't certain himself. Bottom line, it appeared he'd messed up and had just found out about it. Not in his career, he was secure in his position with the Navy. No, this was personal. He'd created it and now he'd have to figure a way to deal with it, and soon.

He sat back, resting his head against the plush leather seat turning a can of soda between his hands. If what he'd learned before he left California for his father's wedding was true, he'd created a life-altering situation. Nothing that wouldn't work out, yet nothing he could share with his family, at least not yet. He had to handle this one on his own.

Thank you for taking the time to read Second Summer. If you enjoyed it, please consider telling your friends or posting a short review. Word of mouth is an author's best friend and much appreciated.

Please join my reader's group to be notified of my New Releases at:
www.shirleendavies.com

I care about quality, so if you find something in error, please contact me via email at:
shirleen@shirleendavies.com

About the Author

Shirleen Davies writes romance—historical, contemporary, and romantic suspense. She grew up in Southern California, attended Oregon State University, and has degrees from San Diego State University and the University of Maryland. During the day she provides consulting services to small and mid-sized businesses. But her real passion is writing emotionally charged stories of flawed people who find redemption through love and acceptance. She now lives with her husband in a beautiful town in northern Arizona.

I love to hear from my readers.

Send me an Email: shirleen@shirleendavies.com
Visit my Website: www.shirleendavies.com
Sign up to be notified of New Releases:
www.shirleendavies.com/contact-me
Check out all my Books:
www.shirleendavies.com/books.html
Comment on my Blog:
www.shirleendavies.com/blog.html
Follow me on Amazon: www.amazon.com/shirleen-davies/e/b00dw9lusw

Other ways to connect with me:
My Facebook Fan Page:
www.facebook.com/shirleendaviesauthor
Twitter: www.twitter.com/shirleendavies
Pinterest: www.pinterest.com/shirleendavies

Google+: www.gplusid.com/shirleendavies.
Tsu: www.tsu.co/shirleendavies.

Other Books by Shirleen Davies

http://www.shirleendavies.com/books.html

Tougher than the Rest – Book One
MacLarens of Fire Mountain Historical Western Romance Series

"A passionate, fast-paced story set in the untamed western frontier by an exciting new voice in historical romance."

Niall MacLaren is the oldest of four brothers, and the undisputed leader of the family. A widower, and single father, his focus is on building the MacLaren ranch into the largest and most successful in northern Arizona. He is serious about two things—his responsibility to the family and his future marriage to the wealthy, well-connected widow who will secure his place in the territory's destiny.

Katherine is determined to live the life she's dreamed about. With a job waiting for her in the growing town of Los Angeles, California, the young teacher from Philadelphia begins a journey across the United States with only a couple of trunks and her spinster companion. Life is perfect for this adventurous, beautiful young woman, until an accident throws her into the arms of the one man who can destroy it all.

Fighting his growing attraction and strong desire for the beautiful stranger, Niall is more determined than ever to push emotions aside to focus on his goals of wealth and political gain. But looking into the clear, blue eyes of the woman who could ruin everything, Niall discovers he will have to harden his heart and be tougher than he's ever been in his life...Tougher than the Rest.

Faster than the Rest – Book Two
MacLarens of Fire Mountain Historical Western Romance Series

"Headstrong, brash, confident, and complex, the MacLarens of Fire Mountain will captivate you with strong characters set in the wild and rugged western frontier."

Handsome, ruthless, young U.S. Marshal Jamie MacLaren had lost everything—his parents, his family connections, and his childhood sweetheart—but now he's back in Fire Mountain and ready for another chance. Just as he successfully reconnects with his family and starts to rebuild his life, he gets the unexpected and unwanted assignment of rescuing the woman who broke his heart.

Beautiful, wealthy Victoria Wicklin chose money and power over love, but is now fighting for her life—or is she? Who has she become in the seven years since she left Fire Mountain to take up her life in San Francisco? Is she really as innocent as she says?

Marshal MacLaren struggles to learn the truth and do his job, but the past and present lead him in different directions as his heart and brain wage battle. Is Victoria a victim or a villain? Is life offering him another chance, or just another heartbreak?

As Jamie and Victoria struggle to uncover past secrets and come to grips with their shared passion, another danger arises. A life-altering danger that is out of their control and threatens to destroy any chance for a shared future.

Harder than the Rest – Book Three
MacLarens of Fire Mountain Historical Western Romance Series

"They are men you want on your side. Hard, confident, and loyal, the MacLarens of Fire Mountain will seize your attention from the first page."

Will MacLaren is a hardened, plain-speaking bounty hunter. His life centers on finding men guilty of horrendous crimes and making sure justice is done. There is no place in his world for the carefree attitude he carried years before when a tragic event destroyed his dreams.

Amanda is the daughter of a successful Colorado rancher. Determined and proud, she works hard to prove she is as capable as any man and worthy to be her father's heir. When a stranger arrives, her independent nature collides with the strong pull toward the handsome ranch hand. But is he what he seems and could his secrets endanger her as well as her family?

The last thing Will needs is to feel passion for another woman. But Amanda elicits feelings he thought were long buried. Can Will's desire for her change him? Or will the vengeance he seeks against the one man he wants to destroy—a dangerous opponent without a conscious—continue to control his life?

Stronger than the Rest – Book Four
MacLarens of Fire Mountain Historical Western Romance Series

"Smart, tough, and capable, the MacLarens protect their own no matter the odds. Set against America's rugged frontier, the stories of the men from Fire Mountain are complex, fast-paced, and a must read for anyone who enjoys non-stop action and romance."

Drew MacLaren is focused and strong. He has achieved all of his goals except one—to return to the MacLaren ranch and build the best horse breeding program in the west. His successful career as an attorney is about to give way to his ranching roots when a bullet changes everything.

Tess Taylor is the quiet, serious daughter of a Colorado ranch family with dreams of her own. Her shy nature keeps her from developing friendships outside of her close-knit family until Drew enters her life. Their relationship grows. Then a bullet, meant for another, leaves him paralyzed and determined to distance himself from the one woman he's come to love.

Convinced he is no longer the man Tess needs, Drew focuses on regaining the use of his legs and recapturing a life he thought lost. But danger of another kind threatens those he cares about—including Tess—forcing him to rethink his future.

Can Drew overcome the barriers that stand between him, the safety of his friends and family, and a life with the woman he loves? To do it all, he has to be strong. Stronger than the Rest.

Deadlier than the Rest – Book Five
MacLarens of Fire Mountain Historical Western Romance Series

"A passionate, heartwarming story of the iconic MacLarens of Fire Mountain. This captivating historical western romance grabs your attention from the start with an engrossing story encompassing two romances set against the rugged backdrop of the burgeoning western frontier."

Connor MacLaren's search has already stolen eight years of his life. Now he is close to finding what he seeks—Meggie, his missing sister. His quest leads him to the growing city of Salt Lake and an encounter with the most captivating woman he has ever met.

Grace is the third wife of a Mormon farmer, forced into a life far different from what she'd have chosen. Her independent spirit longs for choices governed only by her own heart and mind. To achieve her dreams, she must hide behind secrets and half-truths, even as her heart pulls her towards the ruggedly handsome Connor.

Known as cool and uncompromising, Connor MacLaren lives by a few, firm rules that have served him well and kept him alive. However, danger stalks Connor, even to the front range of the beautiful Wasatch Mountains, threatening those he cares about and impacting his ability to find his sister.

Can Connor protect himself from those who seek his death? Will his eight-year search lead him to his sister while unlocking the secrets he knows are held tight within Grace, the woman who has captured his heart?

Read this heartening story of duty, honor, passion, and love in book five of the MacLarens of Fire Mountain series.

Wilder than the Rest – Book Six
MacLarens of Fire Mountain Historical Western Romance Series

"A captivating historical western romance set in the burgeoning and treacherous city of San Francisco. Go along for the ride in this gripping story that seizes your attention from the very first page."

"If you're a reader who wants to discover an entire family of characters you can fall in love with, this is the series for you." – Authors to Watch

Pierce is a rough man, but happy in his new life as a Special Agent. Tasked with defending the rights of the federal government, Pierce is a cunning gunslinger always ready to tackle the next job. That is, until he finds out that his new job involves Mollie Jamison.

Mollie can be a lot to handle. Headstrong and independent, Mollie has chosen a life of danger and intrigue guaranteed to prove her liquor-loving father wrong. She will make something of herself, and no one, not even arrogant Pierce MacLaren, will stand in her way.

A secret mission brings them together, but will their attraction to each other prove deadly in their hunt for justice? The payoff for success is high, much higher than any assignment either has taken before. But will the damage to their hearts and souls be too much to bear? Can Pierce and Mollie find a way to overcome their misgivings and work together as one?

Second Summer – Book One
MacLarens of Fire Mountain Contemporary Romance Series

"In this passionate Contemporary Romance, author Shirleen Davies introduces her readers to the modern day MacLarens starting with Heath MacLaren, the head of the family."

The Chairman of both the MacLaren Cattle Co. and MacLaren Land Development, Heath MacLaren is a success professionally—his personal life is another matter.

Following a divorce after a long, loveless marriage, Heath spends his time with women who are beautiful and passionate, yet unable to provide what he longs for . . .

Heath has never experienced love even though he witnesses it every day between his younger brother, Jace, and wife, Caroline. He wants what they have, yet spends his time with women too young to understand what drives him and too focused on themselves to be true companions.

It's been two years since Annie's husband died, leaving her to build a new life. He was her soul mate and confidante. She has no desire to find a replacement, yet longs for male friendship.

Annie's closest friend in Fire Mountain, Caroline MacLaren, is determined to see Annie come out of her shell after almost two years of mourning. A chance meeting with Heath turns into an offer to be a part of the MacLaren Foundation Board and an opportunity for a life outside her home sanctuary which has also become her prison. The platonic friendship that builds between Annie and Heath points to a future where each may rely on the other without the bonds a romance would entail.

However, without consciously seeking it, each yearns for more . . .

The MacLaren Development Company is booming with Heath at the helm. His meetings at a partner company with the young, beautiful marketing director, who makes no secret of her desire for him, are a temptation. But is she the type of woman he truly wants?

Annie's acceptance of the deep, yet passionless, friendship with Heath sustains her, lulling her to believe it is all she needs. At least until Heath drops a bombshell, forcing Annie to realize that what she took for friendship is actually a deep, lasting love. One she doesn't want to lose.

Each must decide to settle—or fight for it all.

Hard Landing – Book Two
MacLarens of Fire Mountain Contemporary Romance Series

Trey MacLaren is a confident, poised Navy pilot. He's focused, loyal, ethical, and a natural leader. He is also on his way to what he hopes will be a lasting relationship and marriage with fellow pilot, Jesse Evans.

Jesse has always been driven. Her graduation from the Naval Academy and acceptance into the pilot training program are all she thought she wanted—until she discovered love with Trey MacLaren

Trey and Jesse's lives are filled with fast flying, friends, and the demands of their military careers. Lives each has settled into with a passion. At least until the day Trey receives a letter that could change his and Jesse's lives forever.

It's been over two years since Trey has seen the woman in Pensacola. Her unexpected letter stuns him and pushes Jesse into a tailspin from which she might not pull back.

Each must make a choice. Will the choice Trey makes cause him to lose Jesse forever? Will she follow her heart or her head as she fights for a chance to save the love she's found? Will their independent decisions collide, forcing them to give up on a life together?

One More Day – Book Three
MacLarens of Fire Mountain Contemporary Romance Series

Cameron "Cam" Sinclair is smart, driven, and dedicated, with an easygoing temperament that belies his strong will and the personal ambitions he holds close. Besides his family, his job as head of IT at the MacLaren Cattle Company and his position as a Search and Rescue volunteer are all he needs to make him happy. At least that's what he thinks until he meets, and is instantly drawn to, fellow SAR volunteer, Lainey Devlin.

Lainey is compassionate, independent, and ready to break away from her manipulative and controlling fiancé. Just as her decision is made, she's called into a major search and rescue effort, where once again, her path crosses with the intriguing, and much too handsome, Cam Sinclair. But Lainey's plans are set. An opportunity to buy a flourishing preschool in northern Arizona is her chance to make a fresh start, and nothing, not even her fierce attraction to Cam Sinclair, will impede her plans.

As Lainey begins to settle into her new life, an unexpected danger arises —threats from an unknown assailant—someone who doesn't believe she belongs in Fire Mountain. The more Lainey begins to love her new home, the greater the danger becomes. Can she accept the help and protection Cam offers while ignoring her consuming desire for him?

Even if Lainey accepts her attraction to Cam, will he ever be able to come to terms with his own driving ambition and allow himself to consider a different life than the one he's always pictured? A life with the one woman who offers more than he'd ever hoped to find?

All Your Nights – Book Four
MacLarens of Fire Mountain Contemporary Romance Series

"Romance, adventure, cowboys, suspense—everything you want in a contemporary western romance novel."

Kade Taylor likes living on the edge. As an undercover agent for the DEA and a former Special Ops team member, his current assignment seems tame—keep tabs on a bookish Ph.D. candidate the agency believes is connected to a ruthless drug cartel.

Brooke Sinclair is weeks away from obtaining her goal of a doctoral degree. She spends time finalizing her presentation and relaxing with another student who seems to want nothing more than her friendship. That's fine with Brooke. Her last serious relationship ended in a broken engagement.

Her future is set, safe and peaceful, just as she's always planned—until Agent Taylor informs her she's under suspicion for illegal drug activities.

Kade and his DEA team obtain evidence which exonerates Brooke while placing her in danger from those who sought to use her. As Kade races to take down the drug cartel while protecting Brooke, he must also find common ground with the former suspect—a woman he desires with increasing intensity.

At odds with her better judgment, Brooke finds the more time she spends with Kade, the more she's attracted to the complex, multi-faceted agent. But Kade holds secrets he knows Brooke will never understand or accept.

Can Kade keep Brooke safe while coming to terms with his past, or will he stay silent, ruining any future with the woman his heart can't let go?

Always Love You– Book Five
MacLarens of Fire Mountain Contemporary Romance Series

"Romance, adventure, motorcycles, cowboys, suspense—everything you want in a contemporary western romance novel."

Eric Sinclair loves his bachelor status. His work at MacLaren Enterprises leaves him with plenty of time to ride his horse as well as his Harley…and date beautiful women without a thought to commitment.

Amber Anderson is the new person at MacLaren Enterprises. Her passion for marketing landed her what she believes to be the perfect job—until she steps into her first meeting to find the man she left, but still loves, sitting at the management table—his disdain for her clear.

Eric won't allow the past to taint his professional behavior, nor will he repeat his mistakes with Amber, even though love for her pulses through him as strong as ever.

As they strive to mold a working relationship, unexpected danger confronts those close to them, pitting the MacLarens and Sinclairs against an evil who stalks one member but threatens them all.

Eric can't get the memories of their passionate past out of his mind, while Amber wrestles with feelings she thought long buried. Will they be able to put the past behind them to reclaim the love lost years before?

Hearts Don't Lie– Book Six
MacLarens of Fire Mountain Contemporary Romance Series

Mitch MacLaren has reasons for avoiding relationships, and in his opinion, they're pretty darn good. As the new president of RTC Bucking Bulls, difficult challenges occur daily. He certainly doesn't need another one in the form of a fiery, blue-eyed, redhead.

Dana Ballard's new job forces her to work with the one MacLaren who can't seem to get over himself and lighten up. Their verbal sparring is second nature and entertaining until the night of Mitch's departure when he surprises her with a dare she doesn't refuse.

With his assignment in Fire Mountain over, Mitch is free to return to Montana and run the business his father helped start. The glitch in his enthusiasm has to do with one irreversible mistake—the dare Dana didn't ignore. Now, for reasons that confound him, he just can't let it go.

Working together is a circumstance neither wants, but both must accept. As their attraction grows, so do the accidents and strange illnesses of the animals RTC depends on to stay in business. Mitch's total focus should be on finding the reasons and people behind the incidents. Instead, he finds himself torn between his unwanted desire for Dana and the business which is his life.

In his mind, a simple proposition can solve one problem. Will Dana make the smart move and walk away? Or take the gamble and expose her heart?

No Getting Over You– Book Seven
MacLarens of Fire Mountain Contemporary Romance Series

Cassie MacLaren has come a long way since being dumped by her long-time boyfriend, a man she believed to be her future. Successful in her job at MacLaren Enterprises, dreaming of one day leading one of the divisions, she's moved on to start a new relationship, having little time to dwell on past mistakes.

Matt Garner loves his job as rodeo representative for Double Ace Bucking Stock. Busy days and constant travel leave no time for anything more than the occasional short-term relationship—which is just the way he likes it. He's come to accept the regret of leaving the woman he loved for the pro rodeo circuit. The future is set for both, until a chance meeting ignites long buried emotions neither is willing to face.

Forced to work together, their attraction grows, even as multiple arson fires threaten Cassie's new home of Cold Creek, Colorado. Although Cassie believes the danger from the fires is remote, she knows the danger Matt poses to her heart is real.

While fighting his renewed feelings for Cassie, Matt focuses on a new and unexpected opportunity offered by MacLaren Enterprises—an opportunity that will put him on a direct collision course with Cassie.

Will pride and self-preservation control their future? Or will one be strong enough to make the first move, risking everything, including their heart?

Redemption's Edge – Book One
Redemption Mountain – Historical Western Romance Series

"A heartwarming, passionate story of loss, forgiveness, and redemption set in the untamed frontier during the tumultuous years following the Civil War. Ms. Davies' engaging and complex characters draw you in from the start, creating an exciting introduction to this new historical western romance series."

"Redemption's Edge is a strong and engaging introduction to her new historical western romance series."

Dax Pelletier is ready for a new life, far away from the one he left behind in Savannah following the South's devastating defeat in the Civil War. The ex-Confederate general wants nothing more to do with commanding men and confronting the tough truths of leadership.

Rachel Davenport possesses skills unlike those of her Boston socialite peers—skills honed as a nurse in field hospitals during the Civil War. Eschewing her northeastern suitors and changed by the carnage she's seen, Rachel decides to accept her uncle's invitation to assist him at his clinic in the dangerous and wild frontier of Montana.

Now a Texas Ranger, a promise to a friend takes Dax and his brother, Luke, to the untamed territory of Montana. He'll fulfill his oath and return to Austin, at least that's what he believes.

The small town of Splendor is what Rachel needs after life in a large city. In a few short months, she's grown to love the people as well as the majestic beauty of the untamed frontier. She's settled into a life unlike any she has ever thought possible.

Thinking his battle days are over, he now faces dangers of a different kind—one by those from his past who seek vengeance, and another from Rachel, the woman who's captured his heart.

Wildfire Creek – Book Two
Redemption Mountain – Historical Western Romance Series

"A passionate story of rebuilding lives, working to find a place in the wild frontier, and building new lives in the years following the American Civil War. A rugged,

heartwarming story of choices and love in the continuing saga of Redemption Mountain."

Luke Pelletier is settling into his new life as a rancher and occasional Pinkerton Agent, leaving his past as an ex-Confederate major and Texas Ranger far behind. He wants nothing more than to work the ranch, charm the ladies, and live a life of carefree bachelorhood.

Ginny Sorensen has accepted her responsibility as the sole provider for herself and her younger sister. The desire to continue their journey to Oregon is crushed when the need for food and shelter keeps them in the growing frontier town of Splendor, Montana, forcing Ginny to accept work as a server in the local saloon.

Luke has never met a woman as lovely and unspoiled as Ginny. He longs to know her, yet fears his wild ways and unsettled nature aren't what she deserves. She's a girl you marry, but that is nowhere in Luke's plans.

Complicating their tenuous friendship, a twist in circumstances forces Ginny closer to the man she most wants to avoid—the man who can destroy her dreams, and who's captured her heart.

Believing his bachelor status firm, Luke moves from danger to adventure, never dreaming each step he takes brings him closer to his true destiny and a life much different from what he imagines.

Sunrise Ridge – Book Three
**Redemption Mountain – Historical Western
Romance Series**

*"The author has a talent for bringing the historical
west to life, realistically and vividly, and doesn't shy
away from some of the harder aspects of frontier life,
even though it's fiction. Recommended to readers who
like sweeping western historical romances that are
grounded with memorable, likeable characters and a
strong sense of place."*

Noah Brandt is a successful blacksmith and
businessman in Splendor, Montana, with few ties to his
past as an ex-Union Army major and sharpshooter.
Quiet and hardworking, his biggest challenge is
controlling his strong desire for a woman he believes is
beyond his reach.

Abigail Tolbert is tired of being under her father's
thumb while at the same time, being pushed away by
the one man she desires. Determined to build a new life
outside the control of her wealthy father, she finds work
and sets out to shape a life on her own terms.

Noah has made too many mistakes with Abby to
have any hope of getting her back. Even with the
changes in her life, including the distance she's built
with her father, he can't keep himself from believing
he'll never be good enough to claim her.

Unexpected dangers, including a twist of fate for
Abby, change both their lives, making the tentative

steps they've taken to build a relationship a distant hope. As Noah battles his past as well as the threats to Abby, she fights for a future with the only man she will ever love.

Dixie Moon – Book Four
Redemption Mountain – Historical Western Romance Series

Gabe Evans is a man of his word with strong convictions and steadfast loyalty. As the sheriff of Splendor, Montana, the ex-Union Colonel and oldest of four boys from an affluent family, Gabe understands the meaning of responsibility. The last thing he wants is another commitment—especially of the female variety.

Until he meets Lena Campanel...

Lena's past is one she intends to keep buried. Overcoming a childhood of setbacks and obstacles, she and her friend, Nick, have succeeded in creating a life of financial success and devout loyalty to one another.

When an unexpected death leaves Gabe the sole heir of a considerable estate, partnering with Nick and Lena is a lucrative decision...forcing Gabe and Lena to work together. As their desire grows, Lena refuses to let down her guard, vowing to keep her past hidden—even from a perfect man like Gabe.

But secrets never stay buried...

When revealed, Gabe realizes Lena's secrets are deeper than he ever imagined. For a man of his character, deception and lies of omission aren't negotiable. Will he be able to forgive the deceit? Or is the damage too great to ever repair?

Survivor Pass – Book Five
Redemption Mountain – Historical Western Romance Series

He thought he'd found a quiet life…
Cash Coulter settled into a life far removed from his days of fighting for the South and crossing the country as a bounty hunter. Now a deputy sheriff, Cash wants nothing more than to buy some land, raise cattle, and build a simple life in the frontier town of Splendor, Montana. But his whole world shifts when his gaze lands on the most captivating woman he's ever seen. And the feeling appears to be mutual.

But nothing is as it seems…
Alison McGrath moved from her home in Kentucky to the rugged mountains of Montana for one reason—to find the man responsible for murdering her brother. Despite using a false identity to avoid any tie to her brother's name, the citizens of Splendor have no intention of sharing their knowledge about the bank robbery which killed her only sibling. Alison knows her circle of lies can't end well, and her growing for Cash threatens to weaken the revenge which drives her.

And the troubles are mounting…

There is danger surrounding them both—men who seek vengeance as a way to silence the past…by any means necessary.

Reclaiming Love – Book One, A Novella
Peregrine Bay – Contemporary Romance Series

Adam Monroe has seen his share of setbacks. Now he's back in Peregrine Bay, looking for a new life and second chance.

Julia Kerrigan's life rebounded after the sudden betrayal of the one man she ever loved. As president of a success real estate company, she's built a new life and future, pushing the painful past behind her.

Adam's reason for accepting the job as the town's new Police Chief can be explained in one word—Julia. He wants her back and will do whatever is necessary to achieve his goal, even knowing his biggest hurdle is the woman he still loves.

As they begin to reconnect, a terrible scandal breaks loose with Julia and Adam at the center.

Will the threat to their lives and reputations destroy their fledgling romance? Can Adam identify and eliminate the danger to Julia before he's had a chance to reclaim her love?

Our Kind of Love – Book Two
Peregrine Bay – Contemporary Romance Series

Selena Kerrigan is content with a life filled with work and family, never feeling the need to take a chance on a relationship—until she steps into a social world inhabited by a man with dark hair and penetrating blue eyes. Eyes that are fixed on her.

Lincoln Caldwell is a man satisfied with his life. Transitioning from an enviable career as a Navy SEAL to becoming a successful entrepreneur, his days focus on growing his security firm, spending his nights with whomever he chooses. Committing to one woman isn't on the horizon—until a captivating woman with caramel eyes sends his personal life into a tailspin.

Believing her identity remains a secret, Selena returns to work, ready to forget about running away from the bed she never should have gone near. She's prepared to put the colossal error, as well as the man she'll never see again, behind her.

Too bad the object of her lapse in judgment doesn't feel the same.

Linc is good at tracking his targets, and Selena is now at the top of his list. It's amazing how a pair of sandals and only a first name can say so much.

As he pursues the woman he can't rid from his mind, a series of cyber-attacks hit his business, threatening its hard-won success. Worse, and unbeknownst to most, Linc harbors a secret—one with the potential to alter his life, along with those he's close to, in ways he could never imagine.

Our Kind of Love, Book Two in the Peregrine Bay Contemporary Romance series, is a full-length novel with an HEA and no cliffhanger.

Colin's Quest – Book One
MacLarens of Boundary Mountain – Historical Western Romance Series

For An Undying Love...
When Colin MacLaren headed west on a wagon train, he hoped to find adventure and perhaps a little danger in untamed California. He never expected to meet the girl he would love forever. He also never expected her to be the daughter of his family's age-old enemy, but Sarah was a MacGregor and the anger he anticipated soon became a reality. Her father would not be swayed, vehemently refusing to allow marriage to a MacLaren.

Time Has No Effect...
Forced apart for five years, Sarah never forgot Colin—nor did she give up on his promise to come for her. Carrying the brooch he gave her as proof of their secret betrothal, she scans the trail from California, waiting for Colin to claim her. Unfortunately, her father has other plans.

And Enemies Hold No Power.

Nothing can stop Colin from locating Sarah. Not outlaws, runaways, or miles of difficult trails. However, reuniting is only the beginning. Together they must find the courage to fight the men who would keep them apart—and conquer the challenge of uniting two independent hearts.

Find all of my books at:
http://www.shirleendavies.com/books.html

For permission requests, contact the publisher.
Avalanche Ranch Press, LLC
PO Box 12618
Prescott, AZ 86304

Second Summer is a work of fiction. Names, characters,
places, and incidents are either products of the author's
imagination or used facetiously. Any resemblance to
actual events, locales, or persons, living or dead, is
wholly coincidental.

Made in the USA
San Bernardino, CA
14 May 2016